BIGGLES AND THE
LITTLE GREEN GOD

How does the little green god find its way to
Petticoat Lane, London, where Sam Bates
picks it up off a junk stall for eighty pence?
Long afterwards, spurred on by a friend's
casual remark, Sam takes it to a Regent
Street jeweller who realizes its true value and
buys it for £12,500. From time to time we
hear of it changing hands until finally it is
knocked down to a South American multi-
millionaire for £75,000. Its new owner gets
it flown home at once to his house in Santiago,
Chile.
Biggles and Algy now enter the story and we
find them following the route of the aircraft
which never reached its destination.

CAPTAIN W. E. JOHNS

BIGGLES AND THE LITTLE GREEN GOD

KNIGHT BOOKS
the paperback division of Brockhampton Press

ISBN 0 340 13480 1

This edition first published 1971 by Knight Books,
the paperback division of Brockhampton Press, Leicester
Second impression 1974

Printed and bound in Great Britain by
Cox & Wyman Ltd, London,
Reading and Fakenham

First published by Brockhampton Press Ltd 1969
Copyright © by W. E. Johns (Publications) Ltd 1969

CONTENTS

CHAPTER 1

NOT LOST
BUT FAR FROM HOME

BENEATH the intense blue sky of illimitable space only one thing moved. With the world to itself it appeared to dawdle so slowly across the face of heaven that it might have been a microscopic insect that had set itself the impossible task of crawling across the roof of outer space. Alone in a universe from which all life had vanished it was as conspicuous as a fly on a whitewashed ceiling.

In fact, it was an aircraft. To be specific, a twin-engined *Merlin* on the establishment of the Air Police at Scotland Yard, London, England. With its altimeter registering 24,000 feet it was droning its solitary way due west.

Below, rolling away in a shimmering heat-haze to the eastern horizon was a flat plain, a grim landscape of low shrub, rock and sand, that comprises much of the hinterland of Argentina. Ahead, looking across the aircraft's course like the end of the earth was the formidable chain of snow-capped giants that form the mighty Andes, their icy flanks glittering like broken glass, blue, green and crystal white, their lower slopes merging into a purple fantasy of deep shadows marked here and there by the vertical stripe of a torrent of melting snow that plunged down from the frozen world above.

At one point a volcano announced its presence in solemn but spectacular majesty. Every twenty seconds, with the punctuality of a chronometer it belched a plume of yellow sulphurous smoke towards the stratosphere, there to lose itself and disperse slowly in the direction of the unseen stars.

Beyond the mountains, as yet concealed from the eyes of the two men in the cockpit of the plane, Air Detective-Inspector 'Biggles' Bigglesworth and Sergeant-Pilot Algy Lacy, lay the machine's destination, the long, narrow strip of the Republic of Chile, nearly three thousand miles from north to south yet only just over a hundred miles wide, with the Pacific Ocean stretching away beyond to the lost horizons of far distant shores.

Somewhere below the plane, although the pilots could not hope or expect to see it, was a notice board, painted red, on one side the word Argentina and on the other side, Chile. This was the official boundary mark of the two countries.

Somewhere, too, still a long way ahead, beyond the mountains, lay the *Merlin*'s ultimate objective, the airport of Los Cerrilos that serves Santiago, the capital of Chile, seven miles from the city and perched seventeen hundred feet above sea level.

From the altitude to which the *Merlin* had climbed to clear the tremendous obstacle that lay across its course nothing on the ground could be seen in any detail. There was no outstanding landmark, except the erupting volcano which, being one of many perhaps normally dormant, could not be identified by name and therefore served no useful purpose even though it may have been noted on the map of the country. There was no sign or indication of human life. The pilots might have been looking down on a section of the moon's surface. Indeed, it seemed almost impossible that a land so apparently inhospitable could support a population, and this, to some extent, was true: but both knew that in the high tops of this remote region still dwelt the descendants of the original native inhabitants, never really conquered, wild yet dignified, their expressions revealing nothing of their thoughts after centuries of being governed – and in the early days maltreated – by white men from what was to them another world; Europe, a world of which they knew nothing and in which they had no interest.

The plane droned on through an atmosphere that was becoming more and more unstable as it neared the mountains. Both pilots looked often and long at the ground below as if they were searching for something, as in fact they were. So far they had seen no sign of what they sought, although this, in the circumstances, did not surprise them. An aircraft, particularly a broken one, is a very small mark indeed in open country, much less in a world as vast and chaotic as the one below. But Biggles, his eyes for ever going to his compass, knew they were on course and was satisfied that his navigational ability was reliable.

Presently, noticing Algy staring down with a look of concentration on his face he said: 'What are you looking at?'

'Nothing in particular. Just looking,' Algy answered simply.

'See anything?'

'Nothing of the remotest interest to us in our search.'

Biggles went on. 'I thought there was just a chance we might spot something as we crossed the plains, before I started climbing. I wouldn't hold out much hope for the rest of the trip even if it's there. What isn't virgin forest on the lower ground will I imagine be nothing but broken rock. I'm going to climb a little higher to take plenty of room between those two peaks dead ahead. If I know anything the air near them will be turbulent and we're likely to hit some stinking bumps. Feel as if you need a sniff of oxygen? It might freshen you up in more ways than one.'

'No thanks. I'm okay, though it was decent of you to think of it.'

The *Merlin* rocked on through the rarefied atmosphere towards the eternally ice-capped peaks that towered in its path like sentinels guarding the entrance to the polar regions of a dead planet.

By this time the reader will no doubt be wondering for what possible reason an aircraft of the British Air Police could be operating over foreign territory so far from its base. To discover this it will be necessary to turn back the clock for six weeks and begin the operation where it really started, in London, at Police Headquarters, Scotland Yard.

CHAPTER 2

THE AIR COMMODORE'S TALE

'You've proved yourself singularly adept at solving mysteries, Bigglesworth, I wonder what you could make of the one that has just been handed to me?' Air Commodore Raymond, chief of the Special Aviation Section at Scotland Yard, sat back in the chair behind his desk and considered his senior operational pilot with a suspicion of a twinkle in his eyes. In a mildly bantering voice he went on: 'I have a feeling that you like being confronted with a Chinese puzzle which nobody else seems able to solve.'

'You couldn't be more wrong, sir,' replied Biggles, a trifle coldly. 'It has been my fate to scramble through life jumping from one problem to another. They give me sleepless nights, and the only reason I have anything to do with them is because in my youth I was taught to obey orders; and here you give the orders. One of these days I shall come to my senses, buy a little plot of land in Cornwall and grow violets for a living.'

'When that day comes, Bigglesworth, if it ever does, I shall know you're about ripe for a mental home,' rejoined the Air Commodore, sadly. 'I hope it won't happen yet because I've been presented with as pretty a little riddle as you ever heard, and I thought it might amuse you to help me out with it. Still, never mind, if you don't feel like it.'

'You're deliberately provoking my curiosity,' protested Biggles. 'I've fallen for that line before, but now, like an old cock sparrow, I look hard at a trip before I take a peck at it. However, I can listen.'

'That's better,' the Air Commodore said, approvingly.

'When, just now, you mentioned a *Chinese* puzzle, I trust you were not speaking literally?' Biggles said.

'Could be.'

'In that case, let me say at once, sir, that if there's any idea of my aviating a flying machine to China, my pulses are not exactly throbbing with impatience to set a course for the Far East.'

'Wouldn't you like to hear the story? It's an interesting one, if not entirely original.'

'If you have time to tell it, sir, I should be able to find time to listen.'

'Good. It's a long one. I'll begin at the beginning.'

'That's always a good place to start,' agreed Biggles.

'No doubt you will have heard a well-known piece of poetry, a regular party piece, entitled The Green Eye of the Little Yellow God?'

'And a crazy ass known as Mad Carew who tried to pinch it. Oh yes, I know it. Too well. A fellow in my squadron, after a few drinks on guest night, used to climb on the piano and recite it between hiccups. He was slightly madder than Mad Carew, so I needn't tell you what finally happened to him. Don't say someone else has tried his hand at snatching a little yellow god?'

'You're on the beam, but in this case the god happens to be green, with a single big red eye.'

Biggles shrugged a shoulder. 'The colours are immaterial.

People who fiddle about with other people's gods, no matter what colour they may be, usually get what they deserve. Which particular god was this one?'

'Nobody seems to be quite sure; but he must have been somebody very important.'

'Gods usually are important to the people who create them. What was so special about this one?'

'His eye, only one, set in the middle of his forehead, was a ruby of exceptional dimensions.'

Biggles sighed. 'The old story. When will people learn that if they want their gods left alone they should make them of brass with glass eyes? Then there'd be no temptation to lift them off their pedestals. What was this one made of – gold, I suppose?'

'No. Jade. An exquisite piece of work carved from a solid lump of green jade. Weighs about 2 lb.'

'Where did it start life?'

'The experts can't agree on that.'

'I get the drift. It's been lost and you've been asked to find it.'

'As usual, you've hit the nail right on the head.'

'And nobody knows where it *might* have gone?'

'Right again. By now it could be almost anywhere in the world.'

Biggles smiled lugubriously. 'That's charming. I begin to understand what you mean by a conundrum. With the whole world to play in someone's in for a nice long game of hunt the needle. What a hope! And you say you don't even know where it came from in the first place.'

'That's right. But there is a theory. I'll tell you the entire story and you can form your own opinion. As far as we're concerned it begins in London. In the East End. A strange place, you may think, for an idol to start its career. This is how it happened. You've heard of Petticoat Lane?'

'Of course. The junk market near Aldgate East, open on Sundays, where, they say, you can have your watch pinched at one end of the street and sold back to you at the other end.'

'It isn't quite as bad as that nowadays. However ... one Sunday morning, some time ago, a man named Sam Bates, a cockney, just an ordinary fellow, was strolling through the market looking for a little birthday present for his wife, when his eye fell on a curious object, a sort of ornament, on a stall mixed up with a lot of other odds and ends. He thought it was rather pretty and would look well on the mantelpiece at home. To make the story short he bought it for eighty pence, took it home and stuck it on the shelf. There it remained for I don't know how long. Years. He hadn't a clue as to what it really was. To him it was just a lump of polished stone carved into the shape of an ugly little man sitting cross-legged on his bottom with his hands on his knees. A piece of red glass had been stuck in his forehead. It was hollow behind so that the light shone through it. This gave it a rather sinister expression. That didn't worry the Bates family, to whom the image became known as Old Joe. Sometimes it was given to the kids to play with, to keep them quiet. They used to stand it on the cake at Christmas.'

'I've heard of this sort of thing happening before,' Biggles said. 'I remember, some little time ago, a man buying for his wife what was thought to be a string of black beads. He paid two pounds for it, and it was knocking about the house for years till someone discovered the beads were black pearls.* Not surprisingly, for a whole string of black pearls is prac-

*Black pearls, so called, are not actually black: usually a dark green.

tically unknown, this lucky man got thirty thousand pounds for it from a West-End jeweller.'

'Those pearls may have come from the same place as the green god,' said the Air Commodore. 'I told you the story was not entirely original. But let me go on. This is where Fate takes a hand. One day Sam Bates brought in a friend for a drink. The friend noticed Old Joe squatting there on the shelf, and picking it up remarked, as a joke, that it would be funny if the red eye turned out to be a ruby. That was all. Nothing more was said, but after his friend had gone Bates kept thinking about the possibility. Once the seed had been sown he couldn't get it out of his head. He was a poor man, but he wasn't a fool. For the first time he had a long hard look at the quality of the carving and realized the thing might be worth more than the eighty pence he'd paid for it. He was out of work and could do with some money; so one day he put Old Joe in a shopping bag, took a bus to Regent Street and went into one of the leading jewellers.'

'And asked what Old Joe was worth?' suggested Biggles, who was now following the story with mounting interest.

'Don't jump the gun,' requested the Air Commodore. 'He was a cockney, and cockneys have a reputation for being shrewd. No. He showed his one-eyed god to an assistant and asked how much it would cost to have it cleaned. When the assistant could get his breath he said he would have to ask the manager and took it into the office. Presently the manager came out with a queer expression on his face and asked Bates where he had got the idol. Maybe it was the look in the manager's eyes that gave our cockney friend an inkling of the truth. He said: "That's my business."

' "Would you like to sell it?" inquired the manager.

'Bates said he might if the price was right. The manager

said he would have to think about it and suggested Bates came back the next day when he would make him an offer. It was left like that. Bates went home but was back the following day. The manager said he could offer ten thousand pounds for Old Joe, although he didn't call it that. As I have said, Bates was no fool. He said it was worth more so he wasn't selling at that price. The manager raised the offer to twelve thousand, and finally the sale was made at twelve thousand five hundred. Bates went home walking on air, as the saying is, with a cheque for that amount in his pocket. The story got into the newspapers. Later they reported that the idol had been sold to a private collector for a sum that was not disclosed, but no doubt gave the jeweller a handsome margin of profit.'

'So everybody was happy,' murmured Biggles.

'For the time being,' agreed the Air Commodore. 'But the story doesn't end there, not by a long shot. Naturally, following the publicity, the question arose, how did this jewel find its way to Petticoat Lane, of all places? There's a theory, now generally accepted, about that. In fact, it's hard to find another.'

'What's the theory?' inquired Biggles, reaching for a cigarette.

'This is where we have to delve into history,' informed the Air Commodore. 'You may, or may not, know, that in the eighteenth century the Chinese invaded Burma from the north. Having grabbed the country they made war on India. That, of course, led to trouble with us, and without going into details a war started that went on for years. The man responsible for the hostilities was Theebaw, King of Burma. However, it all ended in 1886 when British troops marched into Mandalay, the capital, and a treaty was signed. Now, for a long time there had been a legend that in the king's palace in Mandalay there was a fabulous treasure.'

Biggles groaned. 'Not another treasure!'

'Don't worry, I'm not going to ask you to look for it,' the Air Commodore said quickly. 'There was no treasure. When the troops entered the palace they found nothing – so they said. If there ever had been a treasure it had vanished. So it was reported officially; but not everyone believed this. An ugly rumour was started that the treasure had been looted and, of course, the British troops were blamed. The story was denied, but by now you'll see what I'm driving at.'

'Was the treasure ever found?'

'Never. But let's face it. The rumour may not have been without foundation. Troops have been known to help themselves to souvenirs. It used to be a fairly common practice; but not so much nowadays. We're talking of a long time ago, and there is a chance that the little green god may have gone into a soldier's knapsack. Mind you, this is only theory. There's no proof that anything of the sort happened, but we must admit it *could* have happened. That, some people believe, was how this particular idol, with a whacking great ruby stuck in its forehead, found its way to England – bearing in mind that Burma has always been famous for its rubies, and the Chinese have always been masters in the art of carving jade. The little green god may be very old indeed.'

Biggles agreed that the theory sounded reasonable.

The Air Commodore went on: 'If it's the correct one we can assume that the soldier who brought the thing home had no idea of its value, and if he had he wouldn't be likely to talk about it, looting being a crime for which he could have been shot. What happened to the thing over the years that followed the campaign we don't know, and are never likely to know. All we know for certain is, it eventually found its way to Petticoat Lane and was offered for sale in a tray of junk without anyone realizing what it was or what it was worth. Actually, Bates, the man who stumbled on the truth, didn't live long enough to enjoy his good fortune. Within a week he had been knocked down by a car and killed. He was out on a spree, spending some of his new-found wealth, so it might be said that the idol was indirectly responsible for his death. Queer, isn't it, how often these outstanding jewels leave a trail of death and disaster behind them. The famous Hope Diamond, for example.'*

'If there is anything queer about this sort of thing I'm not prepared to believe that it is the fault of what, after all, is only a piece of mineral,' Biggles said. 'While the world produces villains who are actuated by a policy of wealth at any price, anything of great value is bound to cause trouble. It may be coincidence, but to me it's a natural consequence. Has it been definitely established that this particular god is of oriental craftsmanship? I mean, is it, for instance, a representation of Buddha?'

'No. That's the only thing against this Burma theory. The idol, call it god if you like, for it is obviously something of the sort, is of no religion known today. It certainly isn't any of the Chinese or Indian deities, Buddha, Brahma, Vishnu . . .'

'Then it still isn't known who or what the thing is or where it started its life?'

'That is correct.'

*This notorious 44 carat diamond of a rare blue colour was long believed to bring misfortune to its owner. It was given by King Louis XVI of France to his queen, Marie Antoinette. Both died on the guillotine. In 1911 it was bought in Paris for £60,000 by a man named Mclean. His son was killed shortly afterwards.

Biggles smiled faintly. 'And now no one knows where it's gone.'

The Air Commodore made a wry face. 'You've said it.'

'How did that happen?'

'It's another story,' the Air Commodore said. 'Would you like to hear it?'

'We might as well have the lot while we're at it.'

'All this talking is making me thirsty. Have a cup of coffee?'

'Thanks.'

The Air Commodore rang for a pot of coffee and two cups.

CHAPTER 3

THE AIR COMMODORE
CONCLUDES

When the coffee had been brought the Air Commodore continued.

'This particular work of art we've been talking about – because that's what it is quite apart from the remarkable jewel that decorates its forehead – has been bought and sold several times since it was brought to light in the East End of London. Always the price paid has gone up, as would be only natural, I suppose, because the thing is unique. The purchaser has always been a private individual. Had it gone into a national museum somewhere no doubt it would have stayed there, safe and secure; but apparently the price it has fetched has been beyond what such institutions can afford to pay. The last time it was sold, by public auction at one of the leading London sale-rooms, it was knocked down for £75,000, which is pretty steep even for what is sometimes called a "collector's" piece.'

Biggles pursed his lips. 'There must have been several bidders to send it up to that sort of figure.'

'Actually, at the finish there were only two.'

'Someone must have wanted it badly. Who got it at the finish?'

'A South American multi-millionaire named Don Carlos Ricardo Pallimo who, as a point of detail, comes from Santiago, in Chile, where he owns a lot of land, although much of his business is abroad.'

'Why would he want a thing like that?'

'Heaven only knows, except that it's a common thing for millionaires to become collectors of rare and therefore precious objects. What they want they can get. Perhaps they don't know what else to do with their money.'

'Vanity,' sneered Biggles. 'That's really what it boils down to. They like to be able to swank they've got something nobody else can afford. Maybe they get a kick out of seeing themselves quoted in the newspapers as connoisseurs of art. However, that's nothing to do with me. If that's what they like it's entirely their own affair. Well, what did Señor Pallimo do with his new baby; or rather, how did he come to lose it? If I had spent that sort of money on something to stick on a shelf in the parlour I'd take thundering good care nobody nicked it.'

'He did his best,' the Air Commodore said. 'That's where the mystery comes in. I don't suppose it occurred to him that somebody might steal it. After all, what use is it? Like a valuable painting, a thief couldn't sell it because if he tried it would instantly be recognized as stolen property.'

'In this case the thief might do what the professional crooks do with this sort of swag. The ruby could be prised out of its setting and cut into smaller pieces.'

'That would knock off most of its value. Besides you can't recut a big ruby. It would fly to pieces. But let me continue the tale by telling you what Don Pallimo did, and I think you'll agree he took all reasonable precautions against losing his new little treasure. He made arrangements for it to be flown home at once to his house in Santiago.'

'How did he do that?'

'He chartered an aircraft to take it.'

Biggles stared. 'Great grief! That must have set him back a pretty penny.'

'Only in proportion to the value of the cargo.'

'How nice to be a millionaire,' murmured Biggles with a trace of sarcasm.

'There's no point in having unlimited money if you don't enjoy the advantage it offers.'

'I suppose so.'

'When I said chartered I may have used the wrong word,' corrected the Air Commodore. 'It so happened that an aircraft, an eight-seater *Caravana* belonging to a Chilean air operating company was standing at London Airport. It had brought over a member of the Chilean Embassy and his family and was going back empty. Apparently Don Pallimo was able to make an arrangement with the company to take a parcel home for him. That wouldn't be very difficult. Pallimo couldn't go himself because he had some unfinished business in Europe. It seems he hadn't much faith in the efficiency of the company because he engaged a man, actually a Chilean or a Peruvian, who wanted to go back to South America, to carry the package personally.'

'The package being the idol, I suppose?'

'Exactly.'

'Was the thing insured?'

'Naturally: with a London firm of insurance brokers.'

'For how much?'

'A hundred thousand pounds.'

'The premium must have cost a bit.'

'No doubt. But I don't suppose Pallimo would mind that. Nothing could replace an object that is in fact irreplaceable.

If the plane went down in the sea the god would be lost for ever, anyway.'

'What sort of man is this Pallimo?'

'I've never met him, but from all accounts he's a gentleman in every sense of the word.'

'Spanish, I presume.'

'Of course. Or Spanish ancestry. He claims that a Pallimo was one of the *conquistadores* who were with Pizarro when he took that part of South America in 1531. That could be true, although I imagine the pure Spanish blood has got a little mixed with the native over the centuries. But let me finish. We now come to the part of the story that concerns us.' The Air Commodore pushed forward the cigarette box. 'The aircraft carrying the god left Heath Row about six weeks ago. It arrived safely at its first port of call, Buenos Aires, Argentina, and was checked and refuelled at the main international airport of Ezeiza. So far everything was in order. It then took off on the last leg of its journey to Santiago. That of course meant flying over the Andes. However, the weather was fine. The pilot had done the trip before and there appeared to be no reason why the machine should run into trouble. European and American air lines do the trip regularly.'

'Are you saying it didn't get through?'

'The plane was never seen again. At all events, it didn't arrive in Santiago.'

'If it's down in the mountains it'll take a bit of finding. I suppose a search has been made for it?'

'Of course. Nothing doing. And there's no indication of what could have happened. The pilot was in touch with ground control for some time. Apparently all was well. Then signals suddenly stopped. The company that owns the plane, as well as machines of the Chilean Air Force, have made a thorough search, but all report no trace. The search has now been called off.'

'And that's how things stand at the moment?'

'Yes. Naturally, Don Pallimo is very upset.'

'So must be the relatives of the missing crew, who can have no interest in a lump of carved jade,' Biggles pointed out with a touch of asperity. 'How many people were in the crew?'

'Four. Two pilots, navigator who was also radio operator, and an air hostess. That doesn't include the man carrying the parcel.'

Biggles stubbed his cigarette. 'Now suppose we come to the sixty-four thousand question. What has all this to do with us?'

'We've been asked to do something about it.'

Biggles nodded. 'I had a feeling that was going to be the answer. Why ask us? If it was one of our machines that had gone west it would be a different matter. I can't see that this has anything to do with us.'

'You're forgetting something. A London firm will have to fork out a little matter of a hundred thousand pounds in insurance. With the country short of cash you may be sure the government doesn't take kindly to the idea of handing over so much British currency to a foreigner. Apart from that, Pallimo isn't the sort of man to give up easily. Maybe that's why he's a millionaire. He has it in his head there's been foul play somewhere.'

'I imagine all he's thinking about is his little green god. If he believes there's been some crooked business he must have a reason for it.'

'If that is so he hasn't mentioned it.'

'The Chilean government wouldn't thank outsiders for poking their nose in.'

'You needn't worry about that. Pallimo could straighten that out if it arose. He's an important man in his own country.'

Biggles' brow furrowed in a frown of surprise. His eyes asked a question which after a pause he put into words. 'Are you seriously suggesting that I fly to South America and undertake a private search for an aircraft that might have lost itself anywhere between the Atlantic Ocean and the Pacific?'

'It isn't quite as bad as that. You may not find it necessary to go as far afield. I thought perhaps you might make a few inquiries nearer home; to start with, anyway.'

'Such as where, for instance?'

'That's up to you. It isn't so much the plane we've been asked to find. That, I agree, is no concern of ours.'

'So it's the little green god that's cast its spell on everyone. Is that it?'

Frankly, yes. Or rather, it's the sum of money that the country would be saved by its recovery. The insurance hasn't been paid yet, pending further investigations. I may say that the insurance company has offered the usual reward of ten per cent, ten thousand pounds, for the safe return of the green masterpiece.'

Biggles' lips parted in a cynical smile. 'Do I get the money if I find Old Joe?'

'You know perfectly well that as a police officer you are not allowed to accept a reward for services rendered.'

'Not exactly an inducement for me to stick my neck out by flying over six thousand miles of salt water and another thousand of tropical jungle backed by the highest mountains in the world.'

'You're being awkward again,' chided the Air Commodore.

'Not without reason. You're reckoning that if I get my teeth in this problem I won't let go till I've got this one-eyed lump of mumbo-jumbo in the bag. Well, let me say I'm getting a bit weary of these do-or-die larks with nothing in the end.'

'Be serious, Bigglesworth,' complained the Air Commodore. 'You might at least give some thought to the problem.'

'I've done that already.'

'And, if it isn't a secret, what is your impression?'

'The whole thing is cockeye.'

'In what way?'

'This is no ordinary theft, if in fact it is a theft. That sticks out a mile.'

'I didn't say it was a theft.'

'That's what Pallimo thinks.'

'Go on.'

'Why should a man steal a thing which he must know perfectly well he couldn't offer for sale without incriminating himself? What could he do with it? Keep it in a box under his bed and have an occasional quiet gloat? I can't see a man in his right mind going to all the trouble and expense of getting it just for that.'

'Come to the point.'

'I fancy there's more to this than anyone – except perhaps Pallimo – suspects. Somebody wanted this idol. Wanted it badly. Why? This person, who so far hasn't appeared in the picture, could have been the man who pushed the price up to what Pallimo had to pay to get it. I imagine he tried to buy it. When that failed, presumably because he hadn't as much money as Pallimo, he resorted to more desperate methods to get it.'

'Are you implying that the disappearance of the aircraft

carrying it was not a normal accident? Is that it?'

'From such evidence as we have, that is what I suspect.'

'What gives you that idea?'

'It isn't only *my* idea. It's obviously what Pallimo thinks, otherwise why should he contemplate foul play? I have a notion that he knows more than he has divulged.'

'He's desperately anxious to recover his new toy. Why should he withhold any information that might lead to its recovery?'

'That's a question I can't answer. And I fancy this thing is more than a toy. Unless I've missed my guess there's some sinister influence at work; which doesn't mean I'm superstitious. There could even be a political angle. Before I knock my pan out on this frolic I'd like to have a heart-to-heart chat with this Don Carlos Pallimo. I'd like to have a look at him, anyhow, to judge the sort of man he really is. Where is he?'

'I don't know. I believe he's on the Continent. They'll know at the Chilean Embassy, where I understand he always leaves a forwarding address. They'll know when he's due back in London.'

'In that case, before jumping into an aircraft and tearing to the other side of the world, I'll drift along to the Embassy to get my clock set right for a start. Would you like me to do that?'

'I'd be glad if you would. Handle the thing anyhow you like. I don't want the Chief Commissioner to think we're doing nothing about it.'

Biggles got up. 'Okay, sir. I'll do that. I'll let you know later if I unearth any dark secrets about this little green gentleman with a red eye.'

'Do you really think there could be something criminal?'

'It wouldn't surprise me. Having been around I know this. Anyone who starts fiddling about with a pagan god is asking for trouble, which could be a dose of poison or a poke in the ribs with a long sharp knife. Mad Carew tried it, and we know what happened to him. See you later, sir.' Biggles went out.

CHAPTER 4

BIGGLES ASKS SOME QUESTIONS

BEFORE leaving the building to begin his investigation
Biggles looked into his own office to collect his hat and tell
his assistant pilot on duty, Algy Lacey, what was afoot.

'Before doing anything else I'm going to try to have a
word with this millionaire-type, Pallimo,' he concluded. 'I'm
hoping they'll be able to tell me at the Chilean Embassy
where he is and when he's expected back in London. He may
be co-operative or he may not. We shall see.'

'And if he isn't?'

'He can go and look for his precious green god himself.'

'Can I do anything?'

'Yes. To save me time you might slip along to London
Airport and find someone who helped to organize this Chilean aircraft, a *Caravana*, for its flight home. Check on the
crew for instance.'

'I'll do that,' promised Algy.

'See you later.' Biggles departed, and outside, to save parking complications, took a taxi to the Chilean Office in
London. There, to his surprise and satisfaction, he learned
that the man he wanted to interview had returned to England the previous day and was now occupying his usual suite

at the Hotel Grande, a Spanish-run establishment, in May-fair. He went straight on to it, announced himself to the receptionist and stated his purpose in being there. Having waited for a few minutes while inquiries were made, he was informed that Don Pallimo would see him right away. A page escorted him to the room, knocked, and opened the door.

Prepared to show his official identification papers Biggles went in and found the man he was anxious to interview standing by the window, smoking a long black cigar, waiting for him.

Don Carlos Ricardo Pallimo looked much as might have been expected of a wealthy Spanish South American. He was a man of about sixty years of age, quietly but ex-pensively dressed in an almost black suit with spotless white linen. He was not big, but carried his slight figure like an aristocrat, which presumably he was. Clean shaven and black-haired, he had a smooth flawless skin the colour of old ivory. His eyes were dark with a shrewd penetrating quality that indicated more than ordinary intelligence. His ex-pression was one of calm self-assurance. He moved easily as he stepped forward to receive his visitor, waving aside the credentials Biggles proffered. When he spoke, in perfect English, his voice was quiet with hardly a trace of accent.

'What can I do for you, Inspector?' he inquired. 'Please sit down.' He indicated a chair.

'Thank you, sir,' accepted Biggles. 'I am a specialist in aviation matters from the Air Police department at Scotland Yard. I have been assigned the duty of investigating the disappearance of a valuable object, acquired by you in this country not long ago, which I understand was lost while *en route* by air from London to your home in South Am-erica.'

'You have been correctly informed,' said Don Pallimo. 'I sent it home by special messenger. I suppose you know what the object was?'

'I know as much as anyone in this country seems to know. It was a carved jade figure with a large ruby inset, believed to be an ancient idol which came originally from the Far East.'

Pallimo's answer surprised Biggles. 'You are partly right. It is an ancient – very ancient – object: a god if you like to call it that. But it is not, and never was, oriental.'

'How do you know that?' Biggles couldn't help asking.

'Never mind how I know. Take it from me I *do* know. It's disappearance has upset me very much and I would give a great deal to get it back. If I could think it was lost for ever, at the bottom of the sea for instance, I wouldn't mind so much. I am more concerned that it does not pass into the hands of another person. That, really, is why I bought it.'

Again, this remarkable admission astonished Biggles. 'I assume there is a reason why you should feel like that about it?'

'Let us call it a personal matter. Now, why do you think I should be able to help you?'

'Well, sir, I had to start making inquiries somewhere and this seemed to be the obvious place. You have said, I believe, that there may have been foul play. Is that correct?'

'Yes.'

'Then am I to take it that you regard the loss of the aeroplane carrying your parcel not to be entirely accidental?'

'That is only a suspicion. I have no proof to offer you!'

'But you must have a reason for thinking that!'

'I have a feeling this is not just a matter of common theft.'

'Why?'

Pallimo hesitated. 'Call it intuition.'

'Foul play is a broad term,' went on Biggles. 'Do you think the plane could have been hijacked? That sort of thing has happened, as no doubt you know.'

'It is not impossible. A valuable object is always a temptation to rogues.'

'When you bought the object at public auction somebody must have been bidding against you to lift the price to what you had to pay.'

'I realized that.'

'Do you know who it was?'

'No. I couldn't see. It was someone sitting behind me.'

'A collector of such objects, perhaps?'

'Quite likely.'

'Have you any suspicion of whom it might have been?'

Again Pallimo hesitated. 'No.'

Biggles tried a new tack. 'Having secured the object, you engaged a man, a courier, to take it to your house in Chile?'

'That is correct.'

'Who was this man?'

'Does it matter?'

'It might.'

'He must have gone down with the plane when it crashed.'

'That is assuming it did crash. There is no proof of that.'

'You can be sure he was a man of irreproachable character, or I would not have entrusted him with a package that was worth so much.'

'You haven't answered my question, sir,' prompted Biggles. 'What was his name?'

'O'Higgins.'

'An Irishman?'

'Originally.'

'What does that mean?'

'He was a direct descendant of the famous Bernado O'Higgins, the soldier and statesman who, in the nineteenth century, as commander of the Chilean Army, liberated Chile from the Spanish Royalists. He became Dictator, but was subsequently deposed and went to live in Peru, where he died.'

'So the O'Higgins whom you entrusted with your valuable purchase was a Peruvian?'

'No. Later, some of the family returned to Chile and settled there. I know them well. I knew José O'Higgins was in London and about to return to Santiago, so I asked him if he would take a parcel home for me and he agreed.'

'You talk of a parcel. What sort of parcel was it?'

'A small cardboard carton tied up in brown paper by string.'

'Wasn't that a bit casual for such a valuable object?'

'The idea was to make it look as if the parcel contained nothing of value. Not an original trick, I know. It has often been done.'

'Did O'Higgins know what the parcel contained?'

'Of course. I told him. I trusted him implicitly.'

'Weren't you in rather a hurry to get it home?'

'Perhaps I was; but I didn't want to leave it about.'

Biggles nodded. 'I can understand that. Now, if I am not taking up too much of your time will you please tell me this. You have said the idol is not of oriental origin. Do you know where it came from?'

'Yes. It came from Chile.'

Biggles' eyes opened wide. 'That *does* surprise me. It

would surprise some of the experts on these matters, too, I'm sure.'

Pallimo smiled cynically. 'Do not believe all the experts say. They have to pretend they know. They attribute anything they don't understand to the Far East. They forget, or they don't know, that there were older civilizations. Long before Europe discovered America there were wonderful cultures there. They, too, could produce works of art. The arrival of Europeans was their ruin. Europe began a methodical war of extermination; but a few of the inhabitants managed to get away and survive.'

'You're referring to the Incas.'

'Not necessarily. They came later. There were great civilizations in South America before the Incas, as excavations are now revealing. These earlier people were superlative craftsmen, working in gold and precious stones. They did not know iron.'

'And this idol –'

'Let us get this right. It was a god, held in the highest reverence.'

'You're sure of that?'

'I should know. I live there. All my life I have been a student of the country's early history. I have mastered the language these early people spoke. I could claim to be the greatest living authority on the first South American civilizations, should I care to do so. I have talked to their descendants. I even know the name of the god they worshipped. It was Atu-Hua, god of the *sierras* – the mountains. Another thing you should understand, while we are on the subject, is this: the boundaries of the South American republics were not always the same as they are today. What is now Chile was once upon a time a much larger country than what it has become.'

'Was it because you recognized the god Atu-Hua that you were so anxious to have it?'

'You might say that was one of the reasons.'

'Was there another?'

'Yes, but I would rather not discuss it. Anything else you want to know?'

'This man O'Higgins. Was he of pure European blood?'

'Naturally, after centuries, there is not much absolutely pure European blood in South America. People intermarry. The great majority of the population is what are called *mestizos*; that is, of mixed blood. O'Higgins was one.'

'Then he might have Inca, or even earlier, native blood in his veins.'

'It is possible. It is nothing to be ashamed of. Why do you ask?'

'It merely occurred to me that he might have more than just a passing interest in the god of his forefathers.'

'That would be natural, would it not?'

Biggles agreed. 'Well, sir, if that's all, and there is nothing more you can tell me, I won't take up any more of your time. I take it you are still anxious to recover your lost property, if that is possible!'

'I would give anything to get it back,' stated Don Pallimo in a voice so definite that Biggles gave him a second look. However, he said no more, and after thanking the Chilean for giving him so much of his time he took his departure and returned to the office at Scotland Yard.

'Well, how did you get on?' queried Algy, who was already there.

'Not too badly,' Biggles answered. 'Don Pallimo told me quite a lot, but I think he could have told me more.'

'You think he's holding something back?'

'I do.'

'But why on earth should he?'

'That's a question I can't answer; but I have a feeling in my bones that there's more to this affair than has so far been divulged. It might even have a political angle. How, I wouldn't try to guess. But you know what these South American republics are like. It doesn't take much to start a revolution. Did you learn anything at the airport?'

'Not a lot, but I picked up one item of information which I fancy will interest you.'

'Let's have it.'

'Pallimo's courier wasn't the only passenger in the machine that disappeared.'

'Is that so?' Biggles said slowly. 'You mean – a paying passenger?'

'Yes.'

'I wonder if Pallimo knows that?'

'Surely, if he knew, he would have told you.'

'One would think so. Yet, perhaps not. This might be the key to something he didn't want to talk about. I felt all along there was something. In fact, he as good as said so. There was one aspect he said he preferred not to discuss; one of the reasons why he was so anxious to recover his lost property. That's what convinces me that there's more to this than the intrinsic value of a lump of jade, however beautifully it may have been carved. Who was this extra passenger? Did you manage to get his name?'

'Yes. There was no secret about that. It was Barrendo. Professor Barrendo. A Chilean authority on early American civilizations. Apparently he'd been over here to give a lecture to some society and was anxious to get back home. Naturally, the air line would be glad to fill another seat.'

'And he, I suppose, went west with the rest of the party.'

'No. He's okay.'

'How did that happen?'

'It's been confirmed that he left the plane at Beunos Aires saying he'd decided to call on a relative there and would continue his journey home later. How lucky can some people be?'

'So lucky that one would almost think they'd been given the gift of second sight,' Biggles commented meaningly.

'You're not suggesting he could have known what was going to happen to the plane!'

'I'm not suggesting anything. I'm merely saying that what some people call luck can be the result of having inside information.' Biggles reached to pick up the telephone.

'What are you going to do?'

'I'm going back to see Pallimo if he's still available. There's a question I'd like to ask him. The more I learn about this case the fishier it smells.'

CHAPTER 5

A THANKLESS
ASSIGNMENT

BIGGLES called the Hotel Grande and asked to be put
through to Don Pallimo's apartment. When he had been
connected he said: 'This is Inspector Bigglesworth here, sir.
There is a question I forgot to ask when I was with you just
now. I'd rather not talk over the telephone. Can you give me
a minute if I come round? It won't take longer than that . . .
Thank you, sir.'

'Shan't be long,' he told Algy, and went out.

In a quarter of an hour he was at the hotel. He found he
was expected, and without delay was taken to the room of
the man he wanted to see.

'Yes, Inspector, what's the question?' asked Pallimo,
cheerfully, as he was shown in.

'Two questions, sir, so I'll come straight to the point,'
Biggles said. 'Did you know there was another passenger on
the plane taking O'Higgins and your parcel to Santiago?'

Pallimo's expression changed abruptly. 'No, I certainly
did not know that,' he answered sharply.

'That's what I thought, or you would have mentioned it
to me. The second question is this. Do you know a man
named Barrendo?'

Pallimo frowned. For an instant he looked startled. 'Yes, I know a man of that name,' he admitted. 'What about him?'

'He was the other passenger on the plane.'

Pallimo stared at Biggles' face. He did not speak.

'I thought you'd like to know,' Biggles said, a little awkwardly, perceiving his news had come as a shock. 'That's all, sir.' He turned to go.

Pallimo found his voice. 'One moment, Inspector,' he said quickly. 'This man Barrendo. Was he still on the plane when it disappeared?'

'No. I understand he left it at Buenos Aires, giving the reason he wanted to call on a relative who presumably lives there.'

'Of course,' breathed Pallimo. 'Of course.'

'Why do you say of course?' prompted Biggles. 'Was this what you expected me to say?'

'It's nothing ... nothing,' answered Pallimo shortly. 'Thank you, Inspector, for this information. Good day to you.'

'You're sure there is nothing else you'd like to tell me?'

'Quite sure.'

'At least tell me this,' requested Biggles. 'Had Barrendo a personal interest in the god –'

'His interest was as great, if not greater, than mine,' broke in Pallimo.

'Could he have been the man who bid against you at the auction?'

'It is possible, and that is as much as I'm prepared to say.'

'You're not forgetting that I'm working on your behalf, trying to recover what you've lost,' reminded Biggles with a hint of reproach. 'Obviously, any information you can give me, no matter how trivial it may seem, could make my task easier.'

'I have nothing more to say.'

'In that case I won't detain you. But before I go will you please tell me this. Do you, or do you not, want me to recover, if possible, this god you call Atu-Hua?'

'I don't care if it is lost for ever; but I'm anxious that no one else should gain possession of it.'

Biggles shrugged. 'As you wish, sir. It's up to you. If you feel like that I wonder you bother to claim the insurance money.'

'I paid the premium so why should I not have that to which I am entitled?'

'You insured the god knowing there was a risk of it being lost, or stolen.'

'Yes.'

'Did you inform the insurance company of the unusual risks they were taking?'

'It is not for me to tell them how to run their business.'

'They may have their own ideas about that,' Biggles pointed out. 'However, I won't waste any more of your time. I take it you'll be here should I want to see you again?'

'I shall not be here. I am going back to Santiago at the earliest possible moment.'

If Biggles was surprised he did not say so, or show it. He took his departure and returned to Scotland Yard. He went straight to the office where he found Algy waiting.

'Well?' queried Algy.

'There's no well about it,' returned Biggles. 'The more I see of this business the less I like it. It begins to stink. I'm more than ever convinced that there's more to it than we've been told. Pallimo knows, but for some reason he won't come into the open. He was shaken when I told him Barrendo was on the plane, but he still wouldn't talk.'

'What are you going to do?'

'I'm going down to see the chief right away; and if I have my way he'll tell whoever handed us this bunch of old rhubarb they can cook it themselves. See you presently. Then we'll have some lunch together.'

Biggles went to the Air Commodore's office and found him working at his desk.

The Air Commodore put down his pen and looked up. 'How have you been getting on?'

'Fairly well, sir. One might say too well,' Biggles answered.

'What's that supposed to mean?'

'I've spent the morning talking, but all I've done is stir up enough muddy water to make it impossible to see the bottom of the can. This case looked tricky from the word go, but now I'm sure of it. There's more behind this little lost god business than Mr Pallimo has led anyone this side of the Atlantic to believe. Take my word for that.'

'Have you seen Pallimo?'

'Yes. He's back from the Continent.'

'What did he say?'

'It's what he *won't* say is the snag. He knows what's behind this affair, but for some reason he intends to keep it to himself.'

'But that's ridiculous! How does he expect us to help him if he won't co-operate?'

'That's a question you'd better ask him, sir. He won't tell me. However, I've learnt enough to convince me that the loss of this little green god was no common theft. There's more than one person involved and I suspect Pallimo knows who they are. The whole thing seems to be tied up to some *mystique*.'

'Tell me what you've found out so far.'

Biggles related the results of his morning's work in some detail. 'I'm beginning to think that somewhere in the background there's a political wangle going on, and this little green gent with a bloodshot eye named Atu-Hua is the king-pin in it.'

'Strange that you should run into the name Barrendo,' the Air Commodore said. 'It cropped up here this morning.'

'How did that happen?'

'I've had a visit from one of the secretaries of the Chilean Embassy. He wanted to know if Barrendo was still in England and, if so, if we could locate him for them.'

'You can now tell him he isn't. He's gone home – or at any rate as far as Buenos Aires. He left here on the same plane as O'Higgins, the man carrying the parcel for Pallimo. Something tells me that *Caravana* was never intended to get to Santiago. Or put it this way. If it did, the parcel wouldn't be on board. May I make a suggestion?'

'Do.'

'Let's forget the whole thing and invite Pallimo to work it out himself.'

'It isn't as simple as that.'

'Why not?'

'Do I have to remind you there's a little matter of a hundred thousand pounds to be taken into account?'

'Pallimo doesn't need the money.'

'That isn't likely to prevent him from claiming it.'

'The claim might be invalid on the grounds that he failed to inform the insurance company of certain exceptional risks. I told him so this morning.'

'Could that be proved?'

'It might be difficult if Pallimo denied any knowledge of exceptional risks,' Biggles had to admit.

The Air Commodore shook his head. 'No. We can't get out of it like that. British insurance companies have a world-wide reputation for paying claims and they wouldn't risk losing it. We can't get away from it. The article was insured. It has been lost. The claim will have to be paid. There's only one way of escaping the liability.'

'How's that?'

'By recovering and producing the article.'

'Great grief! That's a tall order. How are you going to do that?'

'Someone will at least have to make a serious attempt to find it.'

'The someone being me, I suppose?'

The Air Commodore smiled bleakly. 'I must confess that was what I had in mind. It wouldn't be all that difficult to follow the track of the lost plane.'

'Provided it stayed on course, perhaps.'

'Do you think it didn't?'

'If it left the regular route it might be anywhere in the world, by now.'

'Not quite. It wasn't carrying unlimited fuel. It would have to land where petrol and oil were available. There should be a record of that, particularly as the *Caravana* is not a common type of aircraft.'

Biggles was silent, knowing his chief's argument was sound.

'Tell me this,' went on the Air Commodore. 'What did you make of Pallimo?'

'Oh, he was civil enough.'

'A hundred per cent white?'

'I wouldn't go as far as that. He might well have a dash of

colour in him. I'd gamble he's a *mestizo*. Why?'

'Because according to the Chilean secretary who came here this morning this man Barrendo, who has come into the picture, is a half-breed. His mother was Indian. That may account for his outstanding knowledge of local history and native lore. It struck me that there might be common ground there with Pallimo.'

'And the green god?'

'Exactly.'

Biggles lifted a shoulder. 'Could be. Pallimo knows, or knows of, Barrendo. That was obvious to me when I mentioned his name. For a moment he looked shaken. But from the way he shied off the subject I think it would be a waste of time trying to get any more out of him.'

'Then we shall have to manage without him. That leaves us with one alternative. Someone will have to make inquiries in Santiago, or at least in Chile.'

'That's likely to be a complicated business as regards travel facilities, by which I mean flying.'

'I don't think so. When I raised the possibility to that Chilean secretary this morning he raised no difficulties. In fact, he seemed anxious to oblige. I'm sure we can rely on him to make the necessary arrangements. I could put you in touch with a useful contact man, a British business agent, in Santiago. There need be no trouble in Argentina, either. Your papers would show you were merely passing over the country on a direct flight from London to Chile.'

'Then you really want me to go?'

'I'd be glad if you would. You've nothing important on at the moment and it would let the higher authority see we were doing our best.'

Biggles got up. 'Okay, sir. In that case I'd better start making arrangements. Bertie and Ginger are on leave, so I'm having lunch with Algy. I'll see how he feels about it.'

The reader will now understand exactly what the British Air Police *Merlin* was doing at 24,000 feet in Western Argentina, bound for Santiago, Chile, with the formidable chain of snow-capped giants, the Andes, looming across its course like the end of the world.

We can now proceed with the story.

So far there had been no difficulty. The Atlantic crossing had been made in fine weather and with the help of a following wind – the celebrated trade wind of the early mariners. With the aircraft's papers in order, and letters of introduction in Biggles' pocket, their reception at Ezeiza, the international airport of Buenos Aires, had been all that could be desired. After a day's rest, in which discreet inquiries about the missing plane and its crew had yielded nothing not already known, the *Merlin*, with full tanks, had taken off on the last leg of its journey.

For the early part the course lay over lush forests, acres of sugar cane, orange groves, lakes and rivers. Later these gave way to the famous *pampas*, the central plains of shimmering grass with their vast herds of cattle which supply the United Kingdom with much of its beef, this to merge eventually into the dry, dusty, rocky foothills already described.

CHAPTER 6

BIGGLES MAKES A CALL

WITHOUT any incident worthy of note the *Merlin* completed its passage over what must be some of the most breath-taking scenery in the world. The very size of the mountains leaves the spectator with a feeling of wonder at the stupendous magnificence of creation.

It was still only a little after noon when, in fine, warm weather, the aircraft touched its wheels on the dusty landing ground of Los Cerrillos.* There was no difficulty here, either, not even in language, for in Chile English is taught in schools and is therefore commonly spoken. The national language is of course Spanish, but there is a variety of it, a mixture, jokingly called Spanglish.

Biggles made himself known to the airport authorities and was courteously provided with parking accommodation. This done he was left to make his own arrangements. These for the moment were simple enough. He was tempted to ask a few questions at the head office of the company to whom the lost plane belonged, but resisted on the grounds that it might be better at this stage not to let too many people know

---

*Curiously, the word Chile comes from an Indian word meaning cold, although in fact much of the country is tropical, or at least sub-tropical.

what he was doing. Before the day was out he was to learn that this may have been a wise precaution.

'So what's the drill?' inquired Algy.

'I think the first thing would be to sample the local notion of some steak and kidney pudding, or what have you. I'm peckish after our long hop. Then we'll get ourselves fixed up with somewhere to stay. After that we can waffle along to call on the man whom the Air Commodore said might be a useful contact on the spot. A Scot named Mr Thurburn, an agent for several British firms. Apparently he's lived here for most of his life, so he should have the latest gossip at his finger tips.'

'Suits me,' agreed Algy briefly.

They found a taxi, conspicuously marked, as is the rule in Santiago, by a white sign on the windscreen, and asked to be taken to the Hotel Santa Lucia, an establishment which they had been told was good without being too expensive.

A twenty-minute drive took them to the entrance and they were soon booked in. A wash and brush up, and finding lunch was being served they went through to the restaurant. 'There's no great hurry,' Biggles told Algy after they had ordered the recommended dish, the popular national one of *Cazuela de Ave*, which turned out to be an appetizing casserole of chicken with mixed vegetables. 'Mr Thurburn may not be back at his office for some time. I gathered from that attendant at the airport that practically everything, including the shops, closes down from about one o'clock until four.'

'Capital idea,' approved Algy. 'I see you've been doing some homework.'

'Always a good thing when you're going to a country for the first time,' replied Biggles sagely.

Some time later, after coffee and a cigarette, feeling refreshed they walked to the office of the man they wanted to see in the Boulevard Calles Ahumada, in the centre of the town. They were at once shown into his private room, which suggested their visit was not unexpected.

A grey-haired, clean shaven man of about sixty rose from his desk, hand extended. 'So you've managed to find your way here,' he greeted, smiling. 'Sit down and make yourselves comfortable. Like a drink?'

'No thanks. We've just had lunch.'

'Cigarette?'

'Thanks. So you knew we were coming,' Biggles said.

'I had a letter from my head office in London to say you might look in, and if you did would I give you any help in my power. The matter was personal, but the approach had been official from someone at your headquarters. So I am at your service, gentlemen. Now, in what way can I help you?'

'Were you told why we were coming here?' was Biggles' first question.

'I was given to understand you are inquiring into the loss of a package that disappeared with the aircraft in which it was travelling somewhere between Buenos Aires and Santiago. I know about the disappearance of the plane from our English-language newspaper here, the *South Pacific Mail*. That, really, is the extent of my knowledge.'

'Do you know what was in the package?'

'No.'

'Do you know to whom it was consigned?'

'No. Nothing was said in the paper about that. It was only concerned with the plane, which, fortunately, was not carrying a full complement of passengers.'

Biggles changed the subject. 'I imagine you are pretty well in touch with local affairs.'

'Naturally. Having lived here for nearly forty years I know what goes on. I came out here as a young man and liked the country so much that I decided to stay – a decision I must say, I have never regretted. Chile is now my adopted home.'

Biggles went on. 'Do you know a man named Don Carlos Ricardo Pallimo?'

'Of course. I have done business with him. He is one of the most important men in the country.'

'In a few words, how would you describe him?'

'Utterly reliable. Why?' Mr Thurburn's eyebrows went up. 'Is he concerned with your visit here? I can't believe he would do anything –'

'No,' broke in Biggles. 'Nothing like that. It was he who put the parcel on the plane in the care of a Chilean gentleman named O'Higgins, who was on his way home after a lecture tour in England. Do you know anything about him?'

'Only by reputation. He's a quiet, retiring man, more concerned with history and archaeology than business. Don Pallimo would know him well, of course. He was interested in the same subjects, although in a more amateurish way.'

'There was another passenger on the plane, a man who took a seat at the last moment. Don Pallimo didn't know that. When I mentioned it to him he looked – well – upset. I'm pretty sure he knew him, but he wouldn't talk about him.'

'What was this man's name?' questioned Thurburn sharply.

'Barrendo.'

'Ah. Was he on the plane when it disappeared?'

'No. He left it at Buenos Aires.'

'That's a pity.'

'What do you mean by that?'

'I can understand Pallimo being upset. All I can say is, a lot of people here would be relieved if Barrendo had never returned to Chile – and I would be one of them.'

'Why?'

'He's a disturbing influence, to put it mildly.'

'Apparently you know something about him.'

'I do. He's a very rich man with a big financial interest in the Chilean nitrate deposits which form one of our principal exports.'

'What's wrong with that?'

'He also takes an active interest in local politics.'

'And so?' queried Biggles.

Mr Thurburn went to the door, opened it quietly, looked out into the corridor and returning, said: 'One can't be too careful. I wouldn't like it to be known I said this. Perhaps I shouldn't say it. But Barrendo is what might be called something of a firebrand. The stuff dictators are made of . . . the Hitlers and Mussolinis of this world. He's a full half-caste. His mother was an Indian woman, and that, naturally, gives him a big following among the native people in the *sierras*.'

'Is there anything wrong with that?'

'He's a dangerous man. A schemer. He's ruthless and ambitious. If he had his way, if ever he got into power he could, and probably would, turn the country upside down.'

'Why should he do that?'

'I don't know. My own feeling is, like many men of mixed breed he has a chip on his shoulder. He resents being what he is because he believes, quite wrongly, that because he is coloured he is despised by the pure whites. Already he is trying to split the country into two factions, the whites and the Indians. This is a nice, quiet, peaceful country, and we don't want anything of that sort here. I need hardly tell you that in South America a revolution means bloodshed. But this need not concern you.'

'I wouldn't say that,' returned Biggles thoughtfully. 'I find what you have just told us very interesting. I came here like a man groping in the dark for something he can't see but suspects is there. Now I get a faint glimmer of daylight. I suppose Don Pallimo knows all about Barrendo's political activities?'

'Of course.'

'That would account for his reaction when I told him Barrendo was a passenger on the plane taking his parcel home. But I feel there's more to it than meets the eye. What puzzles me is why he should decline to tell me the cause of his anxiety, or even discuss it.'

'It may be he's afraid of precipitating a crisis here. Already there have been distant rumblings.'

'But Barrendo, you say, is in big business. What more does he want?'

'Power. Money isn't enough for some people. If Barrendo could make himself a dictator here no doubt he would take care to retain his business interests, and even widen their scope.'

Biggles thought for a moment. 'You've been very frank with me, sir: I appreciate that, and you may be sure I shall respect your confidence. Now perhaps I could tell you something you don't know, something which may have an important bearing on our problem – yours as well as mine.'

'How can you, a stranger here, tell me anything I don't know about the country?'

'I can tell you what was in the parcel Don Pallimo put on the plane consigned to him in Santiago. It was something he bought in London, and he had to pay a large sum of money for it. Somebody else was after it. It was a carved jade idol with a large ruby inset in it. In England it was thought to have come from the Far East, but Pallimo denied this. He told me it was the all-powerful god of some ancient South American civilization.'

Mr Thurburn was staring. 'Did he mention its name?'

'Atu-Hua.'

The silence that followed these words was almost embarrassing. Mr Thurburn, still staring, moistened his lips.

'I'm sorry if I've said something to upset you,' murmured Biggles.

'You certainly have.' Mr Thurburn seemed to speak with difficulty.

'May I know why?'

Mr Thurburn drew a deep breath. 'In Chile, also in Bolivia and Peru for that matter, it is a part of local lore that the success of the Spanish invaders, five hundred years ago, was due to their seizure of the god Atu-Hua. It is also believed that if ever the god returned to its original home the Europeans would be forced to leave the country.'

'And the Indians believe that?'

'Many do.'

'Would Don Pallimo believe this nonsense?'

'Perhaps not. But that wouldn't matter if the Indians believed it. You see what this could lead to?'

'An Indian uprising?'

'I wouldn't go as far as that. But the man who could produce the god would find himself in a position of great power with the natives.'

'Barrendo, for instance.'

'You've said it.'

Biggles nodded. 'Now I understand what Pallimo meant when he told me he didn't particularly want the god himself, but he was anxious that no one else should have it. Does that make sense to you?'

'Most definitely.'

'What he *really* meant was, he wouldn't want Barrendo to get his hands on Atu-Hua.'

'He couldn't have meant anything else.'

'Then why on earth should he send the thing back to Chile?'

'Perhaps he thought it would be safe with him. He may have thought that if Barrendo did start trouble with the Indians, he, Pallimo, could take the power out of his hands by producing the god. At all events, he must have had a reason.'

'So the big question now is this. Has Barrendo got the idol, or did it disappear with the plane that failed to arrive here?'

'That is now a question of paramount importance for everyone in this part of South America. The name Atu-Hua could be dynamite. There is a hard core of natives who have never forgiven the Spaniards for what they did to them, and if it were known that their ancient god was back in Chile, it could spark off a conflagration. Of course, they are never molested now; indeed, everything is done to improve the conditions in which they live. You may think that what happened here in the time of the conquistadors was a long time ago, and so in fact it was; but it can also happen that natives have long memories where injustice is concerned. Normally they live in the mountains and rarely leave their *rucas*, as their thatched homes are called.'

'What beats me is how Atu-Hua could ever have got to England,' Biggles said.

'I can imagine how that might have happened,' replied Mr Thurburn. 'When the Spanish invaders got possession of it they would send it as a trophy back to Spain, in one of their galleons, with the rest of the treasure they found here. As you know, these treasure ships were often waylaid by British pirates and buccaneers, who looted anything of value and divided it among themselves. What more likely than some ignorant English sea-rover took a fancy to the idol and without having the slightest idea of what it was took it home to England. After that, through the years, anything could have happened to it.'

Biggles agreed. 'When you put it like that it's no longer a mystery. No doubt something like that must have happened.'

'Anyhow, that's all past history,' declared Mr Thurburn. 'What is more important is what, knowing what you know now, are you going to do about it? You might be well advised to forget the whole thing and go home.'

'That would suit me, but it isn't as simple as that,' answered Biggles. 'I was sent here on a special mission and I can't back out of it to suit myself.'

'But what can you do?'

'Frankly, I don't know.' Biggles repeated. 'I just don't know. The last thing I want is to find myself tangled in South American politics. Had Pallimo told me what was really behind all this, I'd have thought twice before accepting the assignment.'

'Perhaps he suspected that, and that was why he didn't tell you.'

'I might call on him. He may now feel like speaking more openly. Where does he live?'

'His house is called the Casa Esmeralda.'

'Where is it?'

'About half-way between here and the airport.'

'And Barrendo? Where's his place?'

'On the same road, a mile or so nearer Santiago. The house stands on a hill. The name is Castel Romello. You can't mistake it. There's always an Indian on duty at the drive gate.'

'Why?'

Mr Thurburn shrugged. 'Ask Barrendo. A sort of house guard, perhaps. All his servants are Indians.'

'What's the idea of that?'

'I could guess; but you can draw your own conclusions.'

'On what sort of terms are Pallimo and Barrendo?'

'They know each other well enough, of course. On the surface there is no actual hostility between them, but as they represent two entirely different classes here, one might say political parties, there can't be any love lost between them.'

'So I imagine.' Biggles scrubbed out his cigarette in the ashtray, and concluded. 'Well, sir, thanks for being so helpful. You've given me plenty to think about. I'll let you know what I decide to do. Meanwhile, I won't take up any more of your time.'

'It's been a pleasure.'

'The pleasure has been mutual. I hope we shall meet again.'

That was the end of the interview.

CHAPTER 7

A WARNING AND
A DECISION

'WELL, what do you make of all that?' asked Algy, when they had left Mr Thurburn and started to walk back to their lodgings.

'What we've just learnt clarifies the matter considerably, without, of course, giving us a clue as to how, where and why, the *Caravana* was caused to disappear. The vital question now is, where is this troublesome little god? Was it on board the plane when it left Buenos Aires, or had Barrendo managed to get possession of it? He wants it, and now we know why. The man who could tell us the answer to that is O'Higgins, the messenger, and we haven't much hope of finding him even if he's still alive, which is most unlikely. The future of Chile now seems to depend on where Atu-Hua is at this moment. It's a sobering thought.'

'It looks more and more as if there was dirty work somewhere on the route,' opined Algy.

Biggles agreed. 'Summed up it all boils down to this. There are two powerful forces at work here. That may mean nothing to us, but the little green god is the key that might unlock a floodgate and let loose a bloodbath. I didn't like this business from the start. Now I like it still less. The man who finds Atu-Hua will have a bomb in his hands, and I must admit I'm beginning to hope it won't be me.'

'That may be; but we were sent here to find out what's become of the thing and the Chief will expect us to carry on.'

'I suppose so. Someone at home is only concerned with saving a hundred thousand nicker, although that's peanuts compared with the value of the thing in this country.'

'So what do we do next? Talking about it isn't likely to help us.'

'Talking about it is the same thing as thinking about it, carried a stage farther. We might go and have a word with Don Pallimo, if he's at home.'

'With what object?'

'If he realizes we know more than he told me, what's at the bottom of this business, he may have second thoughts and come right out into the open. After all, he's the man who started it.'

'I can't see how that would help us,' argued Algy. 'Unless the god is found he'll claim the insurance money. I'd have thought a better plan would be to call on Señor Barrendo. If anyone knows anything, he may be the one.'

'That makes him all the less likely to talk, in which case we would have shown our hand for nothing.'

'Okay. It's up to you. What's the alternative?'

'We could make some sorties in the hope of locating the crash, if in fact the plane is somewhere on the ground. If it isn't, it must have shown up somewhere by now,' Biggles said.

'If the package wasn't in the wreck we'd be no farther forward,' argued Algy. 'Pallimo would still demand the insurance money.'

'It may not sound a nice thing to say, but if the plane went up in flames that would settle any more argument. Neither the jade nor the ruby would survive such heat.'

'If we proved that Atu-Hua no longer existed, Pallimo would have a cast iron claim for the insurance,' Algy pointed out. 'That, as I understand it, is exactly what we're trying to prevent.'

'Better that than having a flare-up that could cost a lot of innocent people their lives. We might be able to persuade Pallimo to drop the claim.'

'I wouldn't reckon on that. Why should he? If he's entitled to the money, let him have it – that's what I say.'

'Fair enough. Let's not argue about it. Whatever we do we shall have to be careful. From what Mr Thurburn tells us both Pallimo and Barrendo are powerful enough to make it awkward for us to stay here. Let's leave it like that. It's too late to do anything more today, but if the weather stays fine tomorrow we could try a spot of aviation.'

By this time they had reached the hotel. They would have gone straight to their rooms, but the receptionist at the desk called: 'Señor Bigglesworth.'

'*Si*,' acknowledged Biggles.

The man held up an envelope. 'A message for you, señor.'

'*Gracias*.' After a glance of surprise at Algy Biggles took the letter, and after looking at the inscription on the envelope tore it open. The message on the single sheet of paper it contained was evidently a short one, for in a moment, without a word, he passed it on to Algy.

It did not take Algy long to read it, either. On the sheet of plain paper had been written, in English, in block capitals: BE ADVISED BY A WELL-WISHER. GO HOME. That was all. There was no address. No signature.

Biggles said, 'Look at the envelope.'

Algy looked. It was addressed simply: *Colonel Biggles-worth.*

Algy grinned. 'So you've been promoted.'

Biggles did not smile. 'There's no stamp. This must have been delivered by hand.' Looking at the receptionist, now going on with his work, he inquired: 'Who brought this letter here?'

The man said he did not know. He had not been on duty at the time. His face was inscrutable.

'Who *was* on duty?' asked Biggles.

The man shrugged an expressive shoulder and said he didn't know that, either. He had found the letter lying on the desk when he came in. He spoke in a manner that suggested he couldn't care.

Biggles was not deceived by this, but he realized there was no point in pressing the question. If the man didn't want to talk, and obviously he didn't, nothing would make him. So to Algy he simply said, quietly: 'Let's go and have a cuppa,' and leading the way to a small table in the lounge beckoned the waiter and ordered tea. When the waiter had gone to fetch it he said to Algy:

'What do you make of this letter?'

'Apparently someone is interested in us.'

'Who?'

'Your guess is as good as mine.'

'Not many people know we're here. Somebody, it seems, knows *why* we're here, and where we're lodging. This letter was delivered while we were out. That rules out Mr Thurburn because he didn't know we had arrived until we walked into his office. Somebody must have seen us land and watched where we went. That person knew me by name.'

'He called you colonel.'

'Forget it. He knew better. To give someone a higher rank than the one to which he's entitled is an old trick to flatter a man's vanity. Surely Pallimo wouldn't have written such a message. Why should he? He knows we're working for him. Why should he tell us to go home? That leaves only one man who might have an interest in us.'

'Barrendo.'

'Right. The last we heard of him he was in Buenos Aires, where he left the plane, although from the way Thurburn spoke he must be home by now. He may not like us being here. The man who wrote that letter may, or may not, wish us well; but he'd rather we were out of the way. I smell a threat in it.'

'You mean, he's trying to scare us off.'

'What else? He's obviously a bit scared himself, of what we may uncover, or why should he bother to write a letter at all?'

'What are you going to do about it?'

Here there was a pause in the conversation while the waiter served the tea. When he had gone Biggles continued: 'One thing I'm not going to do is go home.' He went on. 'There's something about this whole business that doesn't add up. Pallimo told me he didn't particularly want the little green god himself, but he was anxious that no one else should have it. I can't see, therefore, why he should have anything to do with the disappearance of the plane, if there was foul play. Why send the god here, anyway? If he didn't want the thing it would have been a simple matter to dispose of it for good. All he had to do was go to London Bridge and sling it in the river. On the other hand, according to Thurburn, Barrendo would be glad to have the idol because of the power it would give him with the Indian population. If he wanted it, it's hard to see how he could have had a hand in the disappearance of the *Caravana*, because that would defeat his object.'

'Barrendo might have pinched the idol when the plane landed at Buenos Aires. If so, after that he couldn't care what happened to the plane,' offered Algy. 'The loss of the aircraft might have been purely coincidental.'

'But if Barrendo pinched the idol at Buenos Aires, or anywhere else *en route*, O'Higgins, who was carrying it would know it had gone. Surely the first thing he'd do would be to inform Pallimo, or at least complain to the airport authorities that he had been robbed. The indications are that the idol was still on board when the plane left Argentina. So was O'Higgins. We can only assume he died in the crash, if in fact there was a crash, so he can't tell us what happened. No, there's something wrong somewhere. Probably a factor that we know nothing about. As things stand we look like running round in ever increasing circles.'

'Well, what *are* we going to do?'

'First, I feel like going along to the Castel Romello to ascertain if in fact Barrendo has come home. We don't know that for certain.'

'And if he is at home?'

'I'd ask him flatly, to his face, if he wrote this letter; and if so, why? That's something he won't be expecting and it might catch him on one foot.'

'When will you go?'

'Now. There's nothing like having a bash at the iron while it's hot. One visit should tell us how we stand with Barrendo, if nothing else. As the old adage has it, to be forewarned is to be forearmed.'

Algy finished his tea. 'Okay, if that's how you feel. Anything you say. But don't you think, as he lives on the same road, that we should call on Pallimo first?'

'Why?'

'He may not approve of us going to see a man with whom, according to Thurburn, he is not on good terms.'

'All the more reason why we should see Barrendo first: then it wouldn't matter if Pallimo did object. At least we can find out if Barrendo has returned home. We're not on the pay-roll of either of them, so we're free to do as we like. I don't care two hoots about this little one-eyed god, but if I can save the government that pays our wages a hundred thousand nicker, I shall reckon we've done a good job. Let's go.'

They went out and found a taxi in a rank not far away. Said Biggles to the driver: 'Do you know the Castel Romello, the house of Señor Barrendo?'

'*Si*, señor,' answered the man cheerfully.

'Good. Please take us there.'

'*Pronto*, señor.'

They got in the car.

A drive of a few minutes saw them at their destination, an imposing mansion house built in the old Spanish colonial style, standing well back from the road and approached by a drive flanked by cypresses, roses, mimosa and other flowering trees and shrubs. The white-painted gate at the entrance was shut, but as they had been informed, an Indian guard was on duty beside a little sentry-box affair, to open the gate as required, or perhaps to see that no unofficial entry was made. They got out of the taxi. Biggles asked the driver to wait – they would walk the rest of the way. The man, a cheerful fellow, agreed.

Biggles and Algy approached the gate together, whereupon the guard stepped forward to intercept them. He asked their business.

'I have come to see Señor Barrendo, if he is at home,' Biggles said.

'The name?'

'Bigglesworth, from London.'

'Wait.'

'He doesn't believe in wasting words,' murmured Algy as the guard went into his sentry-box and unhooked a telephone that hung there, apparently a house phone. They heard him speak, but couldn't catch what he said. In a minute he was back. Without a word he opened the gate and with a gesture indicated they could enter.

'Not exactly garrulous, is he?' quipped Algy softly as they walked on.

'He may have been told to hold his tongue,' returned Biggles. 'I thought there might be some delay, but from the alacrity with which he let us in, I suspect my name must be known to whoever he spoke to at the house.'

'Barrendo isn't taking any risk of being pestered by strangers.'

'Self-protection is one of the penalties you have to face if you have a lot of money,' Biggles said.

Somebody must have been watching for them, for as they came to the front door an overhead light came on and it was opened. Another Indian-type, in the uniform of a house servant, bowed them into a richly furnished hall, and a man who had been standing on a rug at the far end, evidently waiting for them, came forward. He said, in faultless English, 'My name is Barrendo. Welcome to my humble home, gentlemen. This is indeed a pleasure. I am honoured. Let us go in here.' He ushered them into an expensively but tastefully furnished sitting-room and went on: 'Please sit down and make yourselves comfortable. Can I offer you a glass of something? Sherry perhaps?'

'Not for the moment, thank you,' declined Biggles.

Algy had taken the opportunity of having a good look at the man whom they knew by hearsay but had not previously seen. He was small, lean, clean shaven, with a skin darker than might have been expected, apparently inherited from his Indian mother if what Mr Thurburn had told them was correct. At all events, thought Algy, his behaviour so far had been, like his clothes, immaculate. He had prepared himself for quite a different reception.

CHAPTER 8

BARRENDO GIVES HIS VERSION

BIGGLES, having taken the chair, and a cigarette that had been offered to him, spoke. 'If it isn't a rude question, why should our arrival give you pleasure, Señor Barrendo?'

'I was just thinking of calling you on the telephone when you were announced,' was the surprising reply. 'I would have given myself the honour of calling on you, but decided it might be better to give you a chance to get settled in.'

'Does that mean you wanted to see me about something?'

'I thought you might want to see me. As you have come to my house it seems I was right.'

'Why should you think I might want to see you?'

'About the unfortunate business that brought you here, of course.'

'So you know what that is?'

'I can guess.'

Biggles, who had not been prepared for a conversation quite as frank as this, paused for a moment, not knowing how to go on. He resumed. 'Let us agree that we both wanted to see each other. Apparently you know, or have guessed, why I wanted to see you, but I don't understand why you should want to see me.'

'That can soon be explained. It was merely to warn you, as a visitor to our country, to be careful what you do here; to whom you talk and what you say. Things are not always as peaceful as they may appear. To be perfectly frank, I doubt if you will learn much, so it might be better if you went home before running into trouble.'

'Thank you. That's very kind of you and I appreciate your advice; but we have come a long way, and I intend to stay if only for a little while to see something of your lovely country while I am here. Tell me this. How did you learn we were here?'

'A friend gave me the information. He knew you had arrived.'

'You surprise me, señor. We are known to very few people here. May I ask you who would take such an interest in us?'

'Certainly. There is no reason why it should be a secret. It was Don Carlos Pallimo. He rang me up.'

Whatever answer Biggles had expected it was not this. When he had recovered from his surprise he said, 'I came here to ask you one question in particular; as you have been so open with us I might as well ask it now.' As he spoke he took from his pocket the letter that had been delivered to the hotel. Removing the single sheet of paper from the envelope, with his eyes on Barrendo's face he handed it over. 'Did you write this?' he asked bluntly.

Barrendo read the letter. His eyes opened wide. Staring at Biggles he answered, vehemently: 'I most certainly did not write it. I would not have presumed to take such a liberty.'

'Thank you, señor. That answers my question.'

'Why in heaven's name should I write such a letter?'

'You have just given us similar advice, I might say a warning,' reminded Biggles.

'It is one thing to give advice in person, but a different matter altogether to present, anonymously, what almost amounts to an ultimatum. If I had written such a letter why would I have contemplated getting in personal touch with you?'

Biggles saw the force of this argument. 'Very well,' he said. 'You have been so frank with us that I am tempted to pursue this matter a little further. Would you mind if I asked you a few questions?'

'Proceed, señor. I shall be happy to help you in any way I can.'

'Thank you. May I have that glass of sherry you invited me to have just now?'

'With the greatest of pleasure.' Barrendo poured the three glasses and Biggles continued.

'I will start at the beginning, then we shall see how far we are in accord. Apparently you know Don Pallimo?'

'Naturally. We were both born here. He is a neighbour. We have the same interests.'

'Some little time ago, when he was in London, he acquired a small statue.'

'Yes, I know. I would have liked it myself. In fact, being in London at the time I attended the sale hoping to buy it, but I was not prepared to pay as much as he did, for what, after all, is only a curio.'

For a moment Biggles looked slightly bewildered by this candid admission.

Barrendo went on. 'He is a very rich man, and although I am a collector of Inca and pre-Inca relics, it seemed a lot of money to pay for a single item.'

'So you're a collector?' queried Biggles, really for something to say while he was digesting this information.

'Look around and you'll see some of the things I have managed to pick up,' Barrendo said.

Both Biggles and Algy looked round the room and observed a number of strange-looking objects, mugs, jugs, statuettes and the like, standing on shelves or in cabinets, which they had not previously noticed.

'So you know what Pallimo bought?' asked Biggles.

'Yes. It was a prehistoric object of worship, probably of the period known as the Chauvin culture; a god if you like, named Atu-Hua.'

Looking more and more astonished Biggles went on. 'As Pallimo had not finished his business in Europe he sent his purchase home by plane. No doubt you know that, too.'

'Of course. He gave it to a man he knew to bring here.'

'Do you know this man?'

'Certainly. It was O'Higgins, as you probably know.' Biggles nodded. 'We move in the same circle of society, although he lives in the *sierras* some distance from Santiago. He also is a collector of local antiquities, and has done some excellent work deciphering inscriptions on ancient monuments. He has put one Indian language into writing by composing the alphabet.'

'Did he know what was in the parcel he was carrying?' asked Biggles.

'Yes.'

'How did he know?'

'Pallimo told him; or so he told me.'

'Was that why you took a seat on the same plane?'

'No. That was a coincidence. I had received word that my brother, who lives in Buenos Aires, was critically ill, and I was anxious to get to him as quickly as possible. That was why I was on the plane, and why I left it at Buenos Aires.'

'It was lucky for you that you did.'

'So it seems. I was just in time to see my brother before he died. His death kept me in Buenos Aires for a while, settling his estate, with the result that I have not long been home.'

'Tell me this,' requested Biggles. 'This figure of Atu-Hua. Had it any particular value apart from being a work of art, and, of course, the large ruby that went with it?'

'There is a belief that it possessed unique powers, but that of course is merely superstition.'

'Perhaps not everyone would agree with that.'

Barrendo smiled. 'This is a free republic and people are at liberty to think what they like provided they obey the law of the land. The view I just expressed was my personal opinion. And now, Señor Bigglesworth, as I have answered your questions frankly, perhaps you will now allow me to ask one.'

'I will do my best to answer it,' promised Biggles cordially.

'It is quite simple. What is your interest in Atu-Hua and for what particular reason have you come here?'

'In the idol itself I have no interest whatever beyond establishing that it has definitely been lost. It is really a matter of money. The statue was insured in London for a large sum. Naturally, Don Pallimo is putting in a claim, but the insurance company is unwilling to fulfil its obligation while there is a chance that the thing may turn up somewhere. Apart from that, the British government has an interest. It has to watch how much of its currency goes abroad.'

'Then you are not being employed by Pallimo?'

'Certainly not. I am an official of my government.'

'Charged with finding Atu-Hua?'

'Or ascertaining what has become of it.'

'How do you propose to do that?'

'At present I have confined my efforts to seeking any information that would help to clear up the case, one way or the other. Surely there's no harm in that? I cannot understand why it should put me in any sort of danger, as some people seem to think.'

'It rather seems as if it would suit some people to see that you do not succeed in your purpose.'

'Who, for instance? Can you make any suggestion?'

Barrendo shrugged. 'It's no use asking me. I only know from what goes on here that some people might resent your interference in what they would regard as a purely domestic matter.'

'What sort of people have you in mind?'

'The Araucanian Indians might object. They have not forgotten their ancient gods, and, in fact, they still observe some of the religious rites.'

'Do you?'

Barrendo laughed. 'Me! Good gracious, no! I'm a civilized man – I hope.'

'And that's as far as you can help me?'

'I'm afraid so. I've done all I can.'

'For which, señor, I am much obliged to you.' Biggles got up. 'I won't impose on your hospitality any longer.'

'It has been a pleasure.' Barrendo saw them to the door himself, and in parting shook hands in the most friendly manner.

As they walked back down the drive, now in darkness but moonlit, Algy said: 'Well, how do you feel about all that?'

Biggles shook his head. 'I don't get it. The picture was muddy at the start; now it's murkier than ever. We've been misled by someone, intentionally or otherwise.'

'Someone's telling lies?'

'I wouldn't say that. Not yet, anyway. The people we've spoken to may have been misinformed.'

'Barrendo couldn't have been more helpful, more open and above board.'

'I got that impression, too. If he wasn't telling the truth, and the whole truth as far as he knew it, he must be a past-master in the art of lying convincingly. It's a sad thing, but the older I get the more difficult do I find it to trust any-one.'

'You haven't seen many people yet to trust or distrust. Who are they? Pallimo, Thurburn, and now Barrendo. Which of them is trying to lead us up the garden path?'

'I don't know, but with a little patience we shall eventu-ally find out.'

'Are we going on to see Pallimo?'

'Not tonight. I don't see what more he can tell us. He may not like the idea of our going to see Barrendo. I'd prefer to give myself a little time to think over Barrendo's version of the story. One factor has become evident. All the people so far in the picture, and that includes O'Higgins who carried the parcel, have one thing in common. They all have a pro-found interest in the historical relics of the earliest civi-lizations of this country. They are collectors of such things, and this missing god comes into that category, perhaps to a greater degree than we have reason to suppose. They would all like to possess it. I don't think there's much doubt about that. The question is, are they actuated by historical interest, or is there a more serious purpose behind it? But I have a feeling we've done enough talking. It's time we got down to something practical. Tomorrow we'll have a look at those mountains from up topsides.'

'If they'll let us.'

'Why should anyone want, or try, to prevent us?'

'I don't know, but something tells me we're not popular here. There's someone who would rather we didn't interfere. That letter sent to you at the hotel practically proves it. It was intended to scare us off.'

'If the man who wrote it only knew it, it makes me more than ever determined to get to the bottom of this cockeyed business. I'm going to find out what became of this missing *Caravana*. Threats always put my back up. The thing that worries me is, if we should find the machine down in those fantastic mountains, how are we going to get to it?'

They had now reached the drive gate. The taxi was still there, the driver in his seat, waiting, the Indian guard squatting on a stool in his box.

As they strolled up to the car in the most natural way, without haste, the driver, seeing them coming, started his engine. Algy got in on the nearest side, and Biggles was about to follow when he paused, his attention drawn to a sudden movement on the opposite side of the road. This was open country, but the road was fringed by a straggling hedge of prickly pear. From this two figures had detached themselves and were advancing swiftly on the car. Biggles was not expecting trouble, but there was something furtive about the way they moved that made him suspicious. It was too dark to see anything clearly, but there was just sufficient moonlight to glint on something one of the men held in his hand.

'Watch out,' he snapped tersely to Algy. Then, to the driver as he jumped in: 'Drive on.' He slammed the door behind him.

As the car moved forward, accelerating, there was a patter of footsteps on the road behind it. A firearm cracked. And another. Something smacked against the rear of the car.

Biggles ducked, and pulled Algy down beside him.

The driver acted with commendable presence of mind. He did not need to be told what to do. From the way he put his foot down he may have had experience of this sort of thing. The car leapt forward like a horse under the spur. There were no more shots; or if there were, nothing hit the car.

Biggles said quickly to Algy, 'You all right?'

'Yes. I'm okay,' reported Algy. Then he added, grimly: 'As I was saying just now, there's someone in these parts who doesn't like us.'

'I'm beginning to think you're right,' returned Biggles dryly.

'Who could have set those toughs on to us?'

'If we knew that we should know all the answers.'

'Did you see them?'

'Not enough to be able to recognize them if I saw them again.'

The driver raced on for about half a mile, then slowed down. Sliding aside the glass panel behind him he remarked with cheerful humour: 'Some friends were waiting for you, señoritos.' He laughed as if it were a joke.

'So it seems,' replied Biggles. He did not laugh. In a low voice he said to Algy, 'Well, now that some skunk has set our clock right for us, we shall have to be more careful. I still don't understand it. I can only suppose we've blundered into a very nasty plot of some sort, for someone to go to all this trouble to rub us out. Anyway, now we know where we stand. In the morning, as soon as it's light, we'll get cracking.'

CHAPTER 9

DANGEROUS FLYING

THE surface of the earth below the questing *Merlin* aircraft looked as if it had been left unfinished. Hardly begun, in fact. Merely a chaos of rocks thrown down anyhow, gorges as if the world had split and a series of icy pinnacles that ran from north to south in an unbroken chain like a giant necklace of roughly cut diamonds. The Andes. The backbone of the American continent, nearly five thousand miles long and a hundred miles wide, known south of the isthmus of Panama as the Cordillera and north of it as the Rocky Mountains. The greatest moutain system in the world.

Plateaux, large and small, were common on both sides of the topmost ridge, at all elevations, while at not infrequent intervals a feather of smoke coiled up to reveal the volcanic nature of the vast convulsion. For obvious reasons it is not possible to give the average height of this formidable barrier, but it has been estimated at 13,000 feet, although many of the peaks thrust their frozen, untrodden summits well over 20,000 feet into the thin atmosphere of space.

Passes from one side to the other of this vast rock formation do occur for travellers on foot, but they are few and far between, and as most are narrow and flanked by terrifying precipices where a false step could mean a fall of thousands of feet, they are not lightly to be undertaken. Indeed, it is not

uncommon for a traveller to turn back when he sees the
dizzy path that lies before him. And, it need hardly be said,
only a man with iron nerves and in perfect physical condition could hope to make the crossing through air so
rarefied that breathing becomes difficult and often painful.

For three days Biggles and Algy in the *Merlin* had been
searching this inhospitable section of the earth for the missing *Caravana*, so far without the slightest promise of
success, so the operation was beginning to look more and
more futile.

The method employed had always been the same. First, a
long climb to 20,000 feet to clear the menacing obstacle
ahead, always following what should have been the sched-
uled route of the lost aircraft. Then, having surmounted the
fearful peaks, or on occasion having flown between them, a
long glide down the eastern slopes to the more comfortable
altitude of the tree line, where cascading water replaced the
glaciers of snow and ice and the outposts of tropical forest
had climbed their way up from the equatorial regions far
below. Where it was possible Biggles had done a certain
amount of 'weaving', although there was no reason to suppose that the lost machine should deviate, in the hands of an
experienced pilot, from its normal compass bearing. Algy
could well understand why the official search had been abandoned, the authorities taking the view that there was not
much sense in risking the loss of another aircraft for one that
could never be salvaged even if it was located. The crew
could hardly have survived.

Nevertheless, with all this, there was a peculiar fascination
in looking down on a landscape no one but an air traveller
could have seen. Only twice had any sign of life been observed. The first was a small herd of animals, probably

vacunas, on a small plateau. The other was when one of the great white condors that make their homes in the high tops had come close to inspect them – too close to be comfortable. Biggles had swerved away, aware that there had been reports of these huge birds, which know no fear, having been known to attack aircraft, or any other intruder in their domain.

Even at the best, and the weather had remained fine, knowing what engine failure would mean, the flying involved a certain amount of nervous strain, even though in such an event it might, with luck, be possible to make a long glide down to the open country of Chile or Argentina, depending on which side of the divide the trouble occurred. On the present occasion Biggles was making longer sweeps than usual, really as a forlorn hope, making allowance for the possibility that the *Caravana* could have been off course when it had crashed. For there seemed little doubt that it had crashed. There were places where a small machine in the hands of a capable pilot might have got down without serious damage, but a big passenger machine would have no chance at all.

There were times, and this was one of them, when Biggles did not know whether he was flying over Chilean or Argentina territory, because although the boundary was marked at certain spots on the ground it was not possible to see these insignificant guides from the air.

After a period of the usual haphazard flying Biggles suddenly swung the aircraft round to the west with the remark: 'I've had about enough of this. It's getting us nowhere. Had the *Caravana* crashed in any sort of position where it could have been seen from the air, the Chilean Air Force machines that carried out the first search would have spotted it. We've done our best. I'm going back to base. I shall send word to the Air Commodore that we're wasting our time and might as well come home. He must realize that as well as we do. After all, there's no indication, let alone proof, that the *Caravana* was ever within a hundred miles or more of where we are now.'

Algy did not argue. He simply said: 'That's okay with me. You're in charge. I must say it does seem the whole business seems pretty futile.'

Nothing more was said. Biggles flew on, mostly westward, picking a course through the peaks that rose above the general *massif*. The only unmistakable landmark was the volcano noted on the journey out. It was still 'blowing its top,' as Algy put it, at the same regular intervals.

It was some minutes later, with the *Merlin*, which had been dropping off some altitude to get into a more comfortable atmosphere, down to little more than 10,000 feet, when Algy, who had all the time been scrutinizing the ground, said sharply: 'Hold steady a tick. I think I spotted a movement.'

'Where?'

'You see that long flat plateau below the cliff. From up here it looks like an alpine lawn.'

Actually, the feature was unmistakable because it was the only one like it in view; a long apparently level strip of ground about half a mile long and a hundred yards wide; a natural shelf cut into the flank of a mountain with a sheer vertical cliff rising on one side, and on the other a fearful precipice that dropped into a gorge so deep that the bottom was lost in blue mist. The colour of the shelf was mostly green, suggesting vegetation, although at the far end there was a red patch that might have been anything. It was not an uncommon formation. They had seen several like it, large and small. This one was about at the limit of the timber-line. Everything above it was stark rock.

Algy went on. 'On the edge of that patch of red stuff, where the ledge runs into forest. Doesn't that look like someone waving? Anyhow, it's moving.'

'Probably a hunting Indian, after chincillas. I can't imagine anyone else being there.'

'He doesn't look like an Indian to me. He's waving again.'

'That doesn't mean anything. There are still people who will wave to a plane where they're few and far between. We're looking for an aircraft. I don't see anything looking like one. To settle any argument I'll go down a bit for a closer look.'

So saying Biggles throttled back and went into a glide towards the shelf, finally flying over it. This called for care because the air between the mountains was unstable and full of eddies, one of which might carry the machine into the rising face of the mountain before the 'bump' could be corrected.

'You do the looking, I'll do the flying,' Biggles said tersely. Tense, with one hand on the throttle and the other on the control column, he went on: 'What do you make of it? I don't like it. I'm not going any lower.'

'It's a man.'

'What sort of man?'

'It's hard to say, but he looks like a white man. He's sitting down now, but he's still flapping a piece of rag as if calling for help. What can we do about it?'

'Nothing,' answered Biggles promptly.

'Have a heart. It might be somebody in trouble.'

'That's his worry. We could soon be in trouble, too, if I tried to get any closer.' By this time the *Merlin* was down to a hundred feet, flying up and down the shelf.

'We ought to do something,' declared Algy. 'The fellow

looks as if he can't stand up; must be sick or something – had an accident, maybe.'

'What do you suggest we do?' inquired Biggles curtly.

'The ground looks as flat as a pancake. I can't see any rocks. How about landing?'

'Are you crazy? Not on your sweet life. I'm not that daft.'

'The wretched fellow might be dying.'

'That's his affair. We didn't put him there. There's nothing we can do about it. I'm going on home.'

'If we do that, leaving that poor devil stranded, I shan't sleep tonight; nor, if I know anything, will you.'

'Great grief! What do you want me to do?'

'You might try landing. It looks safe.'

'It may *look* safe, but I'm not putting my wheels down without being sure. And we can't be sure.'

'I could check it.'

'Check it? How?'

'You could drop me off. There's a brolly in the cabin. I could go down.'

Biggles stared. 'It's time you had your head examined. You must be out of your mind.'

'I could check the ground to see if it's safe for a landing. If it is you could pick me up.'

'And if it isn't, how do you propose to get home?'

'Walk.'

'You don't know what you're talking about. Walk across those mountains? You couldn't do it. It takes a professional guide, using one of the regular passes, all his time to make the crossing.'

'I'd risk it. You could drop me a load of grub from time to time to keep me going.'

'We've tackled some lunatic exercises in our time, but this is the tops,' stated Biggles. 'Forget it.'

'It doesn't seem to have occurred to you that the person down there might be a survivor of the *Caravana*, which may have hit the deck in the vicinity.'

'We'd have seen it.'

'Not if it went into the timber or fell in the gorge.'

'Okay,' Biggles said impatiently. 'It sounds raving mad to me, but have it your way. I don't like the idea of abandoning anyone in this god-forsaken place any more than you do, but I don't feel justified in risking twenty thousand pounds worth of government property, namely, an aircraft, for which I'm responsible, on the off-chance of helping someone who may turn out not to want any help.'

'If I go down you won't be taking much of a risk,' Algy pointed out. 'I'll have a shot at it. If when I get on the carpet I can find a track clear of obstructions, I'll mark it, and you can come in to pick me up. I'll take some grub with me in case I have to walk home.'

'You'd better. You're not likely to find a restaurant on the way, and you won't do any hitch-hiking, that's certain.'

Algy went aft, presently to reappear wearing one of the two parachutes carried for emergencies. Slung on his arm was a heavy bag. 'Okay,' he said. 'You can take me in. I'll have a good look at the ground before I make a signal and you can rely on me not to ask you to take any risks. If I hold my arms out at right angles you'll know it's no use; in which case you can go home and drop me a bundle of food in the morning. There won't be time today. It'll be dark in a couple of hours. If I wave my hands above my head it'll mean the surface is safe for landing, so if you feel like it you can pick me up. I'll mark out the best track. Right! I'm ready. You say when.' Algy opened the door and stood poised.

'I still think it's an imbecile operation. However, good luck,' Biggles said, and prepared for one of the trickiest manoeuvres he had ever attempted, and he had made many. Only years of experience would help him now, in a situation where, as he knew perfectly well, an error of judgment could prove fatal.

He knew what had to be done, and on the face of it, it did not look too difficult. The real hazard lay in what he could not see, and had no means of finding out: the air currents, thermals and 'sinkers', that would almost certainly be present in such broken ground with extremes of temperature above and below. However, as he lined up the aircraft for its run across the length of the plateau, he found conditions not as bad as he had expected. His fear was that a side wind would carry Algy over the yawning chasm on the left hand side of the shelf, for which reason he flew as close as he dared to the cliff that rose sheer on the opposite side. The risk here was a side eddy which, before he could counter it, might carry him close enough to the rock wall to damage a wing tip. That could have only one result.

When the machine was at three thousand feet, flying dead level at a speed only a little above stalling point, he snapped 'Now'. He felt the slight bump as Algy jumped clear and at once slammed the throttle wide open for more speed, which would give him greater control. He caught a fleeting glimpse of the parachute 'mushrooming'. There was no time for his eyes to follow it down; he was too busy getting farther away from the dangerous wall of rock.

When he next looked down, having reached a more comfortable position, he saw Algy on the plateau gathering up his parachute. Watching from a safe distance, 'S' turning to keep the ledge in view, he saw him hurry along to the figure lying on the edge of the red patch, which he now thought must be flowers, probably poppies. He knelt beside it, but only for a minute. Then, leaving his brolly and the bag beside it he began trotting a zigzag course over the length of the plateau. This of course took some time. Once he stooped, and picking up what looked like a rock carried it to one side. It took about a quarter of an hour to complete the survey. Then, dropping a white object, apparently his handkerchief, to act as a marker, he hurried back to where he had left his equipment and raised both arms above his head, his hands moving in a beckoning signal. This done he plucked some dry herbage and put a match to it. A wisp of smoke trickled up. But this, as a wind indicator, served no useful purpose except to indicate that the breeze was variable, not blowing from any fixed direction. But this was only to be expected in such a place.

Biggles drew a deep breath and prepared for the critical part of the operation. He saw there was no time to be lost, for the sun was nearly down to the peaks, and once it fell behind them the light would fade quickly. He did not know whether to be glad or sorry that a landing was possible, for it was obvious that it would be taking a desperate risk, although it was at least a calculated one. But he had to stand by the arrangement that had been made. In fact, he had known from the beginning that whatever the risks involved he would never have considered leaving Algy stranded in such a place.

Having slipped off a little altitude, he repeated the operation already performed for the parachute drop, only this time he took more room to prevent an overrun that would carry him into the timber, which looked like virgin forest, that had managed to climb up from below to the far end of the plateau. Carefully, his lips pressed together in a straight line under the strain, he glided in.

In the event, the landing turned out to be no more difficult than if he had landed on an aerodrome. The machine rocked once or twice as it ran over uneven ground; but that could happen anywhere. On the whole the air was less turbulent than might have been expected in such an exposed position. The wheels swished through some dry grass and he was down, running to a stop not far from where Algy stood watching. He switched off, and having given himself a 'breather' to recover from the suspense of the last few minutes, he climbed down and waited for Algy, now hurrying towards him.

'Great work!' congratulated Algy enthusiastically. 'I was sure you could do it.'

'Then you knew more than I did,' returned Biggles, lugubriously. 'I'm getting too old for this sort of lark. Never ask me to do anything like it again. Well, what news?' he inquired, taking out his cigarette case.

'Tighten your safety belt. I'm going to shake you.'

'After what I've just done nothing will shake me.'

'It's a girl.'

Biggles nearly dropped his cigarette case. 'Say that again! I couldn't have heard you properly.'

'I said it's a girl.'

'You're sure you don't mean one of these modern long-haired lads . . .'

'I'm still able to recognize the female of the species when I see one,' declared Algy tartly.

'What sort is this one? Indian?'

'Nothing like it. She's white, or as near white as makes no difference.'

'What the devil would a white woman be doing here?'

'I wouldn't know. She's in no state to talk. She's unconscious. In fact, I'm not sure she isn't dead. She looks as though she's been dragged through hell backwards.'

'She wasn't dead half an hour ago. She was moving.'

'That may have been a dying effort.'

'Okay. But instead of standing here nattering, let's do something about it.'

'Just a minute. There's something else you should know; and if this doesn't rock you on your heels, nothing ever will.' Algy's voice had taken on a new, curious expression.

'Shoot. I'm listening.'

'She's wearing a uniform.'

'What sort of uniform?'

'Grey. With wings on the breast of her tunic, and a gold wing cypher on her forage cap.'

Biggles' eyes opened wide. 'You mean – a pilot?'

'No. If she isn't an air hostess I've never seen one. A good-looker, too, I'd say, before she got in the mess she's in now.'

'An air hostess!' Enlightenment dawned in Biggles' eyes. 'Great snakes! The *Caravana* carried an air hostess.'

'Brother, you're reading my thoughts,' Algy said.

'Get the medicine chest,' ordered Biggles, tersely.

CHAPTER 10

ASTONISHING NEWS

IT was nearly half an hour, using the restoratives carried in the *Merlin*'s emergency medical kit, before the girl was brought to a condition of consciousness; or to be more accurate, semi-consciousness, for even after her eyes had opened she seemed dazed, and unable to talk, at any rate, coherently. Biggles, knowing it was useless to hurry matters, allowed her to take her time. During this period of waiting, the sun had dropped behind the highest peaks and daylight was beginning to fade in the glow of approaching evening.

All Biggles had said when he first strode up to her, and dropped on his knees, was: 'She's an air hostess all right. Dressed like that I don't see how she could be anything else.' After testing her limbs for broken bones he went on. 'I don't think there's anything seriously wrong with her. No fever. She looks to me as if she's suffering from shock and exhaustion. From the pallor of her face I'd say it's some time since she had anything to eat. We can put that right. Get the primus going and we'll see what some hot meat extract will do. Wretched girl. She must have been through one hell of a time. However, she's still alive; that's the important thing.'

Algy had been right when he remarked she was a 'good-looker' or had been before her present predicament. There was nothing unusual about this because air hostesses are partly selected for their looks and general appearance, apart from intelligence. She was about twenty years old, slight in build, dark eyed, black haired. Her face was thin and deathly pale, with a recently healed cut on one cheek-bone. It looked as if it had not seen soap and water for some time. Her hands were grimy. Her clothes were torn and in disarray. She had lost a shoe and there was mud up to her knees as if she had been floundering about in a bog.

'She must have been here for quite a while,' observed Biggles. 'Poor kid. She's had a tough time. I'm glad we came down. She'd never have got out of this alone.' While speaking he had been spoon-feeding the patient, a sip at a time, from a cup of Bovril Algy had produced.

'What are we going to do?' Algy asked.

'At the moment we can't do more than we are doing.'

'Don't you think we ought to fly her down to Santiago right away?'

'I don't think we should try to move her yet. There's no great hurry. I want to hear what she has to say. If the plane she was in crashed there may be other survivors not far away; and once I'm off this ledge I shan't feel like having another go at getting back on it. I'm for doing all that's necessary while we're here.'

'If we're not off pretty soon we shan't get away today – unless you feel like trying to get off in the dark.'

'In that case we'll wait for the morning.'

'It'll be mighty cold here presently.'

'We can spend the night in the cabin.'

'What if the weather changes?'

'That's a chance we shall have to take.'

'You're hoping she'll soon be able to talk?'

'Of course.'

'What if she can't speak English? Will your Spanish be good enough?'

'She's bound to speak English. One of the languages all air hostesses have to be able to speak is English, no matter what line they work for.' Biggles pointed to the jungle. 'That's the way she came to get here. You can see her track through those red lilies – or whatever the flowers are. The point is, if she was in a plane crash she couldn't have been in it alone, that's certain. Where are the others? There must be the wreck of a plane not far from here. Are the others still with it? We ought to know before we leave. The girl will know the answer to that.'

At this juncture he noticed her eyes were wide open, and, moreover, in them now was the light of full consciousness. She struggled to get up. Biggles gently pressed her back. 'Slowly,' he said. 'Don't worry. We're friends. Drink.' He gave her the cup and she drank the contents greedily. Biggles smiled. 'Hungry?'

She smiled back, wanly. 'Very hungry. No food for long time. How do you come here?'

'By plane. We saw you wave so we landed.'

'You landed – here?' The girl looked astonished, as well she might.

'How did you get here?' inquired Biggles.

'Plane.'

'You crashed?'

'*Si*, señor.'

'What's your name?'

'Conchita. Conchita Gonzales.'

'You were air hostess on the plane?'

'*Si.*'

'Was the plane a *Caravana*, going from Buenos Aires to Santiago?'

'*Si*.'

'We were looking for it. That's why we're here.'

'So I think when I see you yesterday. That's why I came here, so you can see me, in case you come back.'

'Where is your plane?'

Conchita pointed. She was sitting up now. 'In the trees.'

'How far?'

'Not very far. About one kilometre.'

Here there was a pause while Algy gave her another cup of meat extract, and with it now, a few biscuits. They gave her time to eat these; her condition was improving visibly. A little colour had returned to her pallid cheeks, and a bar of chocolate also produced by Algy brought a smile.

'When you are ready I would like to ask you some questions,' Biggles said.

'I am ready,' Conchita answered. 'I feel better for the food and now I can think.' Her pronunciation of English had just sufficient accent to make it attractive.

'Your plane was forced down. Why? How? What went wrong?'

'There was an explosion.'

Biggles' eyes opened wide. 'An explosion? Where?'

'In the cabin or the luggage compartment, it must have been.'

'Have you any idea of what might have caused the explosion?'

'No. It went off at great force as if someone had put a bomb on board. I was thrown to the floor from the seat where I was reading a book. Suddenly the cabin was full of smoke and fumes.'

'Then what happened?'

'I think the plane must have been damaged. We seemed to be out of control. I am much afraid. I crawled forward and could see the Captain, Captain Ibenez, fighting furiously with the controls. I think for a moment he succeeds and tries to get down on this place where we are now. But there was not room. We rush on and crash into the forest down the slope on the other side.'

'And then?'

'All is confusion. Everyone who could move jumps out quickly. I go. The Captain helps me. But the second officer is trapped, and it is some time before we can get him free. The same with Pepe, the navigator, who was sitting at the radio. He was wounded in the head, and unconscious. At the end we are all out. I find my face is cut and my leg hurts, so that I cannot walk properly. It was terrible.'

'The plane did not catch fire?'

'No, all praise to the saints.'

'You were lucky. There must have been plenty of petrol on board.'

'But certainly. We had taken on extra petrol at El Lobitos for the climb over the mountains, also to put down some mail for the district.'

'Where is El Lobitos?'

'On the plain before the mountains, near the boundary of Argentina.'

'What about the passenger in the plane. Señor O'Higgins?'

'He was not with us.'

'Not with you! How was that? He left Buenos Aires with you.'

'Yes, but he got out at El Lobitos.'

'Why? He had booked to Santiago, or so I understand.'

'He said he was feeling ill. He could wait and follow on a later plane.'

'So you had no passengers?'

'Not one, señor.'

'Then there could have been no luggage on board the aircraft.'

'I don't know. The luggage is not my work. But I saw a bag of mail and some small parcels put in.'

'What happened to them?'

'They must still be in the plane. I do not look to see. No one looks, I think. Everyone is too upset. Captain Ibenez was crying. He was a good pilot. It was his first serious crash. He says now he is ruined.'

'Go on, Conchita. Tell me exactly what happened next.'

'When everyone is better we sit and talk. What else can we do? The plane is a complete wreck. It can never fly again. When I say what happened in the cabin the Captain is sure someone must have put a bomb on board. What else could it be? There had been no trouble with the motors. It was all so sudden. There had been no time to make a signal on the radio. We talked of what we should do. We knew a search would be made when we did not arrive, but with the forest so thick we might not be seen. We wait for three days. We hear planes, but no one sees us. Then we have no food left. The Captain decides that he and Alfredo, the second officer, must go for help. It was the only thing to do. I would go with them, but they would not let me because my leg is still bad. Besides, someone must stay with Pepe, who is sick, wounded in the head. The Captain and Alfredo go off. We see or hear no more of them. No help comes.'

'They did not get to Santiago,' informed Biggles. 'What about Pepe? Where is he?'

'I don't know. Many days ago he said he would go off to find food. I think he had gone sick in the head – loco. He went off into the forest and I have not seen him since.'

'So for some time now you have been alone.'

'*Si*, señor.'

'Without food.'

'Nothing. My leg is better, but it still hurts. I can walk a little way. The cut on my face has got well. Then, two days ago when I think I am about finished, something happens.'

'What was that?'

'Some Indians came. A party of men. Hunters, I think. No women. I don't know where they came from. I did not see. Suddenly they are there. They were not men from a town. They looked like wild men from the mountains. But they did no harm to me. They took no notice.'

'Didn't they give you some food?'

'No. They are very excited and talk much among themselves, but not to me. I do not know what they talk about, but at the finish they load themselves with as many things as they can carry from the plane and go away.'

'They took the things from the luggage compartment?'

'Everything they could carry, even pieces of the plane which they could break off. I have not seen them since. Today, when I heard your plane I come to this open place hoping you would see me. It would have been impossible in the forest.'

'Tell me this, Conchita,' requested Biggles seriously. 'Do you know of any possible reason why anyone should want to wreck your plane?'

'No, señor. We carried nothing valuable. It is all a mystery. It could only have been a bomb. The plane could not have broken itself. It was very good flying weather.'

'Thank you, Conchita,' Biggles patted her reassuringly on the arm. 'You can't tell us more than you know. There's nothing more we can do today.' He glanced at the sky, now darkening. 'I'm afraid you'll have to spend another night here, but we can give you a good meal and we'll make you as comfortable as possible in the cabin. In the morning you can take us to the crash. Alfredo may have come back. When we've done that we'll fly you back to Santiago.'

'*Gracias*, señor. I do not know your name.'

'Biggles. That's what my friends call me, and this is Algy.'

'*Bueno*. Now I know.'

They got Conchita to her feet, and helped her, limping, to the plane. Biggles showed her the miniature toilet where she could wash and make herself as tidy as the circumstances allowed. He then followed Algy to the kitchenette, where he had gone to prepare a meal. Outside, darkness, silent, cold and sombre, was falling like a blanket from the sky.

Said Algy, glancing up as Biggles entered, 'Well, what do you make of it now?'

Biggles answered, 'Nothing. What could anyone make of it? The thing doesn't make sense.'

'Do you believe there was a bomb on board?'

'Everyone else thinks so, and they were there. There must have been something of the sort. But why? That's the question. Why would anyone do that? I see it like this. Only three people knew about this dangerous little god being on board. They were Pallimo, O'Higgins and Barrendo. Let's take them one at a time. First Pallimo. Would he, just having paid so much money for a thing, deliberately go out of his way to destroy it, or see that it was dumped where no one would ever find it?'

'One wouldn't think so,' conceded Algy, opening a can of cream of chicken soup.

'Then there's O'Higgins,' continued Biggles. 'He offered to take the thing home. Pallimo regards him as a friend to be trusted. We know he didn't stay in the plane. He got out at this post and refuelling station, El Lobitos. He may have kept Pallimo's parcel with him. But whether he did, or not, what possible reason could he have for preventing the *Caravana* from reaching Santiago? The same with Barrendo. He left the plane at Buenos Aires, and he said why. To see a sick brother. For what earthly reason should he sabotage the aircraft? He may have wanted the idol, but that wasn't the way to get it. If he was responsible for what has happened he's put it out of his reach for ever. No, there's something wrong somewhere.'

'There's one factor you may have overlooked,' Algy said, gently stirring the soup in the saucepan. 'You're assuming that this nasty little one-eyed god, Atu-Hua, was the reason for blowing up the aircraft.'

'What else are we to think? Conchita says there was nothing of value on board.'

'All the same, the explosion may have had nothing whatever to do with Atu-Hua being on board. The skunk who planted the bomb, if it was a bomb, may have known nothing about the god. As you've said, there were only three people in the know. We may get a fresh idea tomorrow when we've had a look at what's left of the *Caravana*. We may find a clue. If Atu-Hua is still there in the luggage, all we have to do is get to Santiago, hand the infernal thing over to its rightful owner and then go the shortest way home.'

'I couldn't agree more,' declared Biggles. 'But I'm bound to say this. If Atu-Hua is still in that wreck it'll surprise me more than anything else so far.'

'You don't think it's there?'

'All the known facts suggest it didn't get as far as this. I may be wrong, but I'd say it disappeared somewhere *en route*.'

'Okay. Let's leave it like that,' suggested Algy. 'Meanwhile, let's have something to eat. Conchita still has a lot of leeway to make up in the grub stakes. How bad is her leg?'

'Nothing serious, as far as I've been able to make out. I fancy she's torn the muscle in her calf. Only time can put that right. It'll be painful for quite a while. She may be limping for weeks. Presently I'll put an elastic bandage on it. That may help. There's nothing more we can do – nothing more anyone else could do.'

'Fair enough. You might get out some bowls and spoons. Holy mackerel, and all the other little fishes! What a way we've chosen to make a living. Serving soup to lost women in a perishing jungle.'

Biggles grinned. 'Pipe down. We haven't finished yet, not by a long chalk. If I know anything this lark has only just begun.'

CHAPTER 11

THE CRASH

THE weather held. The morning after the finding of the stranded air hostess dawned still but cold, and grey under a mantle of mist. But this was soon dispelled by the rising sun and the dome of heaven resumed its immutable serenity of eggshell blue. This put everyone in good heart, for a change of weather in the mountains could have serious consequences. Conchita, after a good night's sleep, and having washed the accumulated grime off herself, looked a different person. Being young she recovered quickly. No doubt her relief at being rescued, when she must have abandoned hope, had something to do with it. She was cheerful as she helped with the chores, although as Biggles had predicted she still walked with a limp. Biggles cut her a strong stick to act as a support for the injured leg.

A substantial breakfast from the stores always carried in the *Merlin*, starting with a base of that universal standby where food is not readily to be had, porridge oats with condensed milk and sugar, and they were set for whatever the day might bring, although fortunately, perhaps, there was as yet no indication of what that was to be.

As they sat finishing their coffee, there being no particular urgency, Conchita asked: 'Why do you want to see the crash? There isn't much to see: only the pieces. They will never send a salvage party here to fetch them.'

'I merely want to check up on something,' replied Biggles. 'Something that may or may not be there. Do you know anything about the ancient Indian gods in these parts?'

'No, señor Biggles. I only know it is better to have nothing to do with them, or even talk about them.'

'Who told you that?'

'My mother. All children are told that. The Indians are peaceable people now, except perhaps on feast days when they get so drunk they don't know what they are doing. Then it is better to keep away from the places where they gather.'

'Do you know the names of any of these old gods?'

'No.'

'So you've never heard of one called Atu-Hua?'

'No. Why?'

'Because somehow, years ago, it found its way to Europe, and was being brought back here in the plane in which you were travelling. This is as far as it got.'

Conchita smiled. 'You will not ask me to believe that a heathen god caused the plane to crash?'

'No, I would not ask you to believe that,' said Biggles.

'But surely you don't believe it yourself?'

Biggles dodged the question. 'It's time we were moving,' he said, getting up. 'The sooner we've done what I want to do, to save coming back here again, the sooner we shall be able to take you home to report what happened. Then the company that owns the plane can do what they like about it. I don't think there's any need for you to come with us. Conchita. You should rest your leg. The more you use it the worse it will be. Just tell us where the crash is, and the best way to get to it, and you can rest here while we're away. We shouldn't be long.'

Conchita objected to this. Her leg, she declared, was better, and she was able to walk. It would, she argued, be difficult to describe exactly where the crash lay. It would be much easier to show them.

Biggles, against his better judgment be it said, for he thought the girl with her injured leg was likely to be an encumbrance, did not press the point. 'Very well,' he said. 'As you wish. Let us be going. The sooner we get away from here the better. I see cloud up from the west and I would not trust the weather to last.'

The matter decided, they were soon on their way, Conchita following her own track through the patch of red lilies to where the forest began. It was thick and damp, and the ground underfoot was slippery with rotting veg- etable matter. The way lay steadily downhill, not directly but at an angle, as if it might have been a game track coming up from, or leading down into, the gorges that yawned below. There were some steep places where Conchita had to be helped, and Algy found himself wondering how she had managed to make her way up to the plateau. He could only conclude that she had been driven by desperation, which probably was the explanation.

After nearly half an hour of slipping and sliding through the green twilight under the tropical trees, with their great evergreen leaves, Conchita said they were nearly there. But for the track she had made in the soft ground on her out- ward journey, it is likely they would all have been lost. But she was right. Another few minutes and they came to the place where the ill-fated aircraft had torn a swathe of nearly a hundred yards through the jungle.

It was a sorry spectacle. Most forms of mechanical

transport that have come to grief on land or sea, still bear some resemblance to their original form; but an aircraft, with lightness in its construction as a first consideration, almost disintegrates when it plunges into the ground. In this case only the fuselage remained more or less intact. The wings had been stripped off and flung back over the cabin, throwing off the engines that had been mounted on them, to show their ribs. They lay strewn about, with undercarriage wheels and pieces of buckled metal and torn leather that had once been seats.

The wreck lay silent in its silent surroundings. None of the crew that had left it had returned, and after what Conchita had told them Biggles would have been surprised to find any of them there. He did not contemplate making a search for them, knowing this would be futile; a waste of time and effort.

As he paused to take stock he observed grimly: 'Anyone who got out of this mess alive was lucky. The trees, Conchita, by catching the wings and absorbing the worst of the shock of impact, may have saved you. You sit down and rest while we go through the cabin and luggage compartment. It shouldn't take long. Come on, Algy, give me a hand.'

In a few minutes it was evident that nothing had survived undamaged. There was nothing whatever in the cabin, so that was soon disposed of. The luggage compartment, in the belly of the fuselage under the cabin floor, had been ripped open from end to end. The mail bag was there, torn open, the letters it had contained lying all over the place. Some of the wrappings of what had been parcels were there, but of their contents there was no sign.

'That must have been done by the Indians who came here,' remarked Biggles. 'Conchita said they made off with everything they could carry. If Atu-Hua was here he'll have disappeared with the rest, this time, I fancy, for ever.' He pointed to some letters, charred at the edges by burning. 'That proves there must have been an explosion of some sort. Conchita was right there. This is where it must have happened. I'm not going to try to work out who put a bomb on board, or why; I've knocked my pan out already sweating over that problem.'

They looked in the cockpit but found nothing of interest there. It was a complete ruin, as if an attempt had been made to tear out the instruments – as Biggles remarked, probably more Indian work.

Oddly enough, the big main petrol tank had not been fractured. 'That's where they were lucky,' Biggles said. 'Had it broken open everything would have gone up in flames and this would have been a different story. Well, that's about all we can do,' he went on in a resigned voice. 'I didn't seriously expect to find Atu-Hua, so I can't say I'm disappointed. At least we shall be able to tell Pallimo that we made a search and found the crash. He can now do what he likes about it. Let's get back to the plateau and call it a day.' They rejoined Conchita where she sat waiting.

'Did you find anything?' she inquired, naturally.

'Nothing,' answered Biggles. 'All we can tell you is, you were right about an explosion. It's unlikely anyone will ever know what caused it, so all we have to do now is see about getting ourselves home. You can take your time. There's no particular hurry. We don't want to make your leg any worse.'

They had stooped to help Conchita to her feet, but she raised a hand. 'Listen! What is that noise?'

From some distance off, below, in the gorge it seemed, came a strange medley of sounds, consisting chiefly of wild singing, or chanting, with occasional yells, accompanied by the throbbing of a drum and the clashing of cymbals.

Biggles frowned. 'That, in a place like this, can only be Indians.'

Nobody disputed this.

Biggles looked at Conchita. 'Did the Indians make this noise when they came here before?'

'No. They came in silence. I did not see them till suddenly they were here. That's why I thought it was a hunting party.'

'Which way did they come?'

'I don't know. But that's the way they went, down the side of the hill.' Conchita pointed.

'Maybe their village is somewhere down in the valley,' surmised Biggles.

'It sounds as if they're coming this way,' put in Algy, as the noise increased in volume.

'That may mean they are coming back here,' Conchita said.

'That wouldn't surprise me,' returned Biggles tersely. 'Looking for anything else worth carting away. But I don't think that they should worry us . . . unless . . .'

'Unless what?' Algy asked the question.

'Unless something has upset them. If it has they may turn nasty. There's no knowing what an Indian will do if he goes off his rocker. It would be as well, I think, to keep out of their way, to be on the safe side. Wait a minute. I'll see if I can see them. Which way they're going. They may not be coming here at all. We don't want to put any unnecessary strain on Conchita's gammy leg by hurrying her. No. I'll tell you what, Algy. It might be better if you started off right away, taking it slowly. 'I'll keep an eye on things and follow you as soon as I've seen what this is all about. I think that's the best plan.'

Conchita got up, and with Algy holding her arm for support started back up the track by which they had come down. Biggles watched them go and then moved slowly towards the edge of the decline that overlooked the gorge. He was anxious, but not particularly alarmed.

The barbaric din was coming closer.

Algy and Conchita pressed on up the damp, sticky track, and soon found that the going up was harder work than the going down. Still, they made fair progress, but coming to a dry patch, seeing Conchita was making heavy weather of it, Algy suggested they sat down for a rest. There appeared to be no need for them to drive themselves to the point of exhaustion. He was thinking, of course, of Conchita's injured leg. It was obvious she was in some pain, and the way she accepted the idea, and sank down, suggested the leg was hurting her more than she pretended. Anyone who has torn a muscle in his calf will understand this.

They sat. They did not talk. There was nothing much to say. They merely sat gazing back in the direction from which Biggles would come. They waited for perhaps ten minutes or a quarter of an hour and they were preparing to move on when they saw him coming; and there was an urgency in the way he was moving that suggested the news he was carrying was not going to be reassuring. Not that there was any reason to expect good news, for the pandemonium of shouts and singing was already coming closer.

'On your feet,' ordered Biggles curtly as he strode up. 'That crazy gang may not come as far as this, but I'm pretty sure they're on their way to the crash. That's too close to be comfortable. I doubt if they really know what they're doing, but in the mood they're in they could get up to any sort of devilment.'

'You've seen them, then?'

'Yes. I got close enough to have a good look at what was going on.'

'What can have come over them?' questioned Conchita, looking puzzled. 'They don't usually behave like this.'

'Now, maybe, they have a reason,' Biggles said. 'They're all dolled up as if for a big occasion – paint on their faces, feathers in their hair, ribbons and all sorts of gimcrack finery. They're being led by a sort of witch-doctor type with something on a pole.'

'With what on a pole?'

'Can't you guess?'

'No. Tell me.'

'Atu-Hua!'

'Atu-Hua,' breathed Algy. 'So that's what all the fuss is about.'

'Evidently. I've never seen this confounded little god, but from the description the thing can't be anything else. I was wrong. Atu-Hua must have been on the plane after all.'

'So they've found him.'

'Why not? He must have been in one of the parcels they took from the wreck.'

'So they've got their god back.'

'Yes, and they obviously intend to make the most of him,' answered Biggles grimly. 'This is what certain people we know may have been afraid of. It could start something.'

'But why have this lot come back to the crash?'

'How would I know? Don't ask me to guess what goes on in the mind of an Indian. But let's not stand talking here. You hurry on and get a couple of pistols out of the magazine. Load them and bring one back here to me, just in case there's trouble. I'll follow on as fast as I can with Conchita.'

Algy did not argue. He walked on, quickly, alone.

Biggles helped Conchita to her feet and they followed more slowly.

CHAPTER 12

DISTURBING EVENTS

BIGGLES and Conchita emerged from the forest on to the open plateau to see Algy, a gun in each hand, coming to meet them.

For a few seconds Biggles paid little attention to him. He was too taken up with what, now he was clear of the trees, was revealed. There had been a marked change in the weather. There was no wind, or rain, but the bright early morning sun had been blotted out by mist, a grey, moisture-soaked, ground mist, which filled the scene and reduced visibility to twenty or thirty yards. The *Merlin* had been enveloped as if in cotton wool and could not be seen.

What had caused this change could only be conjectured, but it is the sort of thing that can happen, and does happen, in mountainous country. It was not heavy rain cloud, so it had probably been caused by a shift in the direction of the wind, bringing in colder air. But what had caused it was not the vital issue. It was the effect. It was evident that while these conditions persisted there could be no question of taking off; at all events, not without taking risks not pleasant to contemplate.

Algy came hurrying up. 'You see what's happened?' he said bitterly. 'We should have pulled out while we had the chance.'

'All right? There's no need to get in a flap,' returned

Biggles, taking one of the pistols and putting it in his pocket. 'It's always easy to see what one *should* have done – after the event. There's been no great harm done, so far. Given the same circumstances I'd do what I did this morning. It was a calculated risk and I decided it was worth taking. Without occasionally taking a risk one doesn't get far in this world. I'm glad I took this one because we now have a piece of important information we would otherwise have missed. We know that this infernal god we're chasing was on board the *Caravana* after all, and we know where he is now. That's something.'

'So what do we do now?'

'The only thing we *can* do. Wait for this stuff to lift or roll away. That could happen any minute.'

'It could also last all day; or, for that matter, two or three days.'

'I'm well aware of it; but there's no need to depress ourselves by looking at the black side.'

'Where are the Indians?'

'From what we can hear I think they must have reached the wreck. If that was their objective they may come no farther. They can't know we're here.'

'What if they *do* come here?'

'We'll deal with that situation if it should happen. I don't believe in trying to jump a fence till I come to it. Meanwhile, how about a nice cup of tea?'

'You won't move the *Merlin*?'

'There's no need. I left it facing the only possible direction for a take-off. If our brown-skinned lunatic brothers come any closer we shall hear them. If that should happen I'll go to meet them. If they turn nasty I'll point out that they should be grateful to us for bringing back their god. They'll suppose we were in the *Caravana*.'

Nothing more was said. They all walked on until the *Merlin* loomed like a ghost in the mist. Algy went in to make a pot of tea. Biggles and Conchita found seats on tufts of grass outside the more easily to judge the whereabouts of the Indians. Biggles lit a cigarette. Conchita accepted one. After what she had already endured she did not appear upset by the situation that had developed. As a professional air woman she must have realized that they were temporarily grounded and nothing could be done about it.

When Algy rejoined them with a jug of tea and some packets of biscuits, the weather conditions were unchanged. The Indians could be heard shouting and singing, but as far as could be judged they had not come any nearer. The conversation lagged. There was nothing to be said. Biggles watched the mist for the first indication of its dispersal.

After a while Algy said: 'I imagine you'll get off as soon as this murk clears enough for us to see what we're doing?'

'I've been thinking about that,' Biggles replied thoughtfully.

Algy looked surprised. 'What is there to think about?'

'I am thinking it would be nice if, when we went, we could take Atu-Hua with us.'

'You must be as crazy as the Indians,' declared Algy. 'What does it matter what happens to that pop-eyed lump of nonsense?'

'If we could recover it, it would save London having to fork out the insurance money to Pallimo.'

'We know it's still in existence.'

'That isn't enough. How could we prove it? Pallimo hasn't got it. Unless he gets it he would be justified in claiming the insurance.'

'I'd leave other people to argue about that.'

'No doubt. When I finish a job I like to leave everything clean and tidy. It's time you knew that.'

Algy shrugged. 'Okay. Have it your way. You're too conscientious, that's your trouble.'

'Call it my misfortune,' countered Biggles. 'Let's not argue about it.'

Algy said no more.

Conchita changed the subject. 'I wish I knew what had happened to Pepe. He was a nice boy. I was fond of him. He helped me much when we first flew together.'

'How old was he?'

'Twenty years.'

'Bad luck. I'm afraid we're not likely to find him,' Biggles said sadly. 'What hope would a man have, alone, of getting out of a place like this?'

'He might find a way. He was part Indian.'

Biggles looked up. 'Well, that might be to his advantage,' he conceded. 'He might know, better than we would, what could be eaten.' He spoke really to comfort Conchita, not because he thought there was really any hope for the missing radio-navigator.

Another silence fell. The tea was finished. Biggles lit another cigarette and counted how many he had left. Time wore on. Then, suddenly there came such an uproar of screams and yells from the direction of the crash that it brought them all to their feet in some alarm.

'What was all that about, I wonder?' muttered Biggles.

'Smoke,' said Conchita, pointing. 'I see smoke. They make a fire.'

'Looks as if they've decided to make a bonfire of what's left of the plane,' observed Algy. 'Maybe in honour of dear old Atu-Hua coming home. There's nothing else to burn; it's all too wet.'

'I hope for their sake they haven't done anything as stupid as that, although I must admit that's what it looks like,' Biggles said as a great mushroom of smoke rolled turgidly above the tree tops on the near edge of the forest.

'What does it matter, anyway,' Algy said shortly. 'The plane's a write-off. Best thing that could happen to it.'

'You seem to be forgetting something.'

'I saw nothing worth the trouble of salvage.'

'That may be. I'm thinking of the petrol. The main tank was intact, as we noticed; which probably saved the plane from going up in flames when it struck. If it goes up now the poor fools will wish they'd made their bonfire somewhere else.'

The words were almost taken out of his mouth by a tremendous explosion that rocked the air, sent birds flying and threw a sheet of flame and debris into the sky.

'There she goes! They've done it,' Biggles said calmly.

Again his words were almost drowned in a pandemonium of screams, shrieks, howls, and the clatter of debris falling back into the trees. The sounds that followed, fast receding, suggested precipitate flight.

'So the silly asses have burnt their fingers,' Algy said.

'I'm afraid some of them may have burnt more than that,' retorted Biggles lugubriously. 'Poor ignorant fools. They couldn't be expected to know what was likely to happen. You stay here. I'll slip down to see what has happened. I can hear groans as if someone has caught a packet.'

'Why bother?' questioned Algy. 'I'd let them fend for themselves. If you attempt to interfere you're likely to get more kicks than thanks. Why let them know we're here?'

'I think any still on their feet have gone,' Biggles said. 'Have the Red Cross box handy. The most likely injuries will be burns.'

'Please yourself, but I think you're making a mistake in going near the thing,' was Algy's opinion.

'Have a heart,' requested Biggles. 'Remember, what's happened down there may happen to us one day.' So saying he turned away and started off at a brisk walk towards the scene of the disaster.

Knowing the way, it did not take him long to reach it. He approached cautiously, because even before it was in sight he could hear moaning, so he knew someone was there even though most of the Indians had fled from the scene of their folly – or perhaps it would be fairer to say, ignorance.

When he did reach the crash he found an even more appalling spectacle than he had expected, although he knew from the force of the explosion that it was bound to be bad. The whole area was littered with smoking debris, rags, feathers and other finery that had been torn from the bodies of the celebrating natives. The fuselage had practically disintegrated, and with its equipment, seats and the like, torn and mutilated, lay scattered far and wide. The remains of the petrol tank was a smouldering heap of twisted metal.

Three bodies lay near it. These men must have been near the tank when it exploded, for their clothes had been stripped from them, and apart from being shockingly burnt they had been slashed by flying metal. One had been impaled by a sliver of steel. A glance was enough to show they were beyond help. A movement caught Biggles' eyes and he saw a man, on the edge of the devastated area, on his hands and knees trying to crawl away. As he hurried to him he observed that his skin was nothing like as dark as the others he had seen.

On his way he tripped and stumbled over a pole that had been dropped in the stampede to get away from the spot. Attached to one end of it by leather thongs was an object which, although he had not mentioned it, he thought might be there. Atu-Hua. Smiling grimly at the thought of the mischief it had brought on its worshippers, he left it lying there and went on to the injured man, who, hearing footsteps, looked over his shoulder and saw Biggles.

He was young. Not much more than a lad. Perhaps twenty years old. '*Socorro!* (help)' he gasped. Biggles did not answer but dropped on his knees to see where, or how badly, he was hurt. The boy, his face twisted with pain, tried to help by lying on his back.

Biggles could find no wound, but saw he had been badly burned on his face and hands. His hair was singed to the scalp. His eyebrows and lashes had disappeared. His body seemed to have escaped, and the reason for this, as Biggles saw with some surprise, was because he had been protected by clothes. They had been scorched, but he could see they were not like the rags the Indians had been wearing. His jacket, with metal buttons and an insignia of some sort on the chest, appeared to be some sort of uniform. Then, to use the common expression, the penny dropped. It *was* a uniform. The man was not an Indian.

'Can you speak English?' he asked sharply.

'Yes, señor. I have English,' was the reply.

'Your uniform. Were you one of the crew of this plane?'

'*Si.*'

'Could you – be Pepe?'

'*Si*. I am Pepe. How you know?'

'Conchita told me.'

'Conchita. Where is she?'

'She is safe.'

'Praise be to God! How you come here?'

'I have a plane. We were searching for you. Conchita waved to us. What were you doing with these Indians?'

'I leave Conchita to look for food. I am nearly dead when they find me and take me to their village. They ask me how I come. I tell them by plane. Then they find plane. There is much excitement. *Fiesta.*'

'Why didn't you stop them making a fire knowing there was so much petrol on board?'

'They were mad. Drunk. They could not understand. They must make a sacrifice because . . .'

'Because they think Atu-Hua has come back to them?'

Pepe looked astonished. 'You know that!'

'Yes. You can tell me more later.' As a matter of fact, although he was only too well aware that Pepe was in urgent need of treatment, he had fired his questions fearing he might lose consciousness, or even die from shock, and the opportunity would be lost. He went on. 'I can't do anything for you here. Can you walk?'

'Walk where?'

'To my plane where I could dress your burns. If you can't walk I must fetch them, leaving you here alone; and the Indians might come back. It would be better if you could walk, if not all the way then part of the way. We must get away from here.'

'I will try,' Pepe said, and struggled to his feet, to stand swaying as if he might faint. He was obviously still suffering from shock and his burns must have been agonizing.

Biggles took him by the arm and they started off. Before leaving the spot he picked up the mud-bespattered idol that had caused so much mischief and carried it under his arm.

CHAPTER 13

REVELATIONS

WITH Pepe hanging heavily on his arm, taking frequent rests, Biggles reached the plateau hoping to find that the mist had dispersed. It had not. Indeed, if anything it looked worse, the thin air so overladen with moisture that it was beginning to fall as a fine drizzle, making everything uncomfortably wet.

Algy and Conchita, who must have been watching, saw them coming and came forward to meet them, Conchita limping on her one sound leg.

'See who's here,' called Biggles cheerfully.

She did not need to be told. 'Pepe!' she cried incredulously, and would have embraced him had Biggles not prevented it, pointing out that he was in no condition for caresses. 'Now now, Conchita,' he said firmly. Then, to Algy, 'Put this thing in the machine out of the way.'

'What is it?'

'Atu-Hua.'

Algy looked shocked. 'Why bring that trouble-making load of rubbish here?'

'We've had enough worry finding it, I thought we might as well keep it. Besides, it may turn out to be a trump card in the maniac game we're playing.'

Nothing more was said for the time being, everyone helping to get the injured radio-operator to the *Merlin*, where Biggles' first treatment was to give him a pill to relieve the pain he was suffering. Then his burns were dressed and bandaged. They could have been worse. Only exposed skin had been affected, and this had been scorched more than blistered. After a cup of soup, for he was obviously in need of food, he declared he was 'as good as new', although this was to be doubted. But once made comfortable in the *Merlin*'s roomy cabin, when the effects of shock began to wear off his condition improved rapidly and he was able to talk coherently.

'You realize we can't get you away while this fog lasts,' Biggles said.

Pepe, of course, understood that.

'While we're waiting you might as well tell us, as far as you know, how all this happened,' Biggles suggested. 'The sooner we know how we stand the better. Besides, it will save time later.'

'What do you want to know?' asked Pepe.

'Several things. But first, do you think the Indians might come back to what's left of your plane?'

Pepe didn't know. 'They might. They don't really know what they're doing. It all depends on the witch-doctor who has them under his thumb.'

'Why did they come back to the *Caravana* when they had already taken away as much as they could carry?'

'To make a sacrifice to the plane for bringing back Atu-Hua. At least, that is how I understood it.'

'What were they going to sacrifice?'

'Me.'

Biggles stared. 'Are you saying they intended to sacrifice you?'

'Yes.'

'How?'

'In the same way their ancestors were sacrificed when white men first came to the country. By burning on a fire.'

'Charming,' murmured Algy.

'Haven't they forgotten that?' queried Biggles.

'They have forgotten nothing. The story is passed from one generation to another. They made a fire of pieces of the plane and were just going to throw me on it when the petrol blew up. I suppose that saved my life. In their hurry to escape they forgot all about me.' Pepe smiled. 'They may have thought Atu-Hua was angry about something.'

'Apparently he was,' put in Algy, softly.

'Tell me this,' requested Biggles. 'Did you know Atu-Hua was on your plane?'

'No. How could I possibly know that? The first I knew of it was when I found their village and found them dancing round him. I say village, but it's more than that. It's an ancient stone ruin, a temple, I think with houses for priests round it. Like some others that have been discovered not long ago. This one, built of the same rock as the mountain is well hidden, and hard to see until you are close to it. I suppose that is why it had never been discovered.'

Biggles nodded. 'Do you know what forced your plane down?'

Pepe hesitated.

'Don't ask me to believe it was Atu-Hua,' bantered Biggles.

'It could have been – in a way.'

'In what way? Conchita tells me there was an explosion.'

'Yes.'

'What caused it?'

'It must have been a bomb.'

'How could a bomb have had anything to do with Atu-Hua?'

'I don't know.'

'How could a bomb have been put in the machine?'

Again Pepe hesitated. 'It was perhaps because Atu-Hua was on board that a bomb was put in. Now that I have had time to think about it, I can see it may have been my fault.'

'*Your* fault!' exclaimed Biggles. 'How on earth could that be?'

'I will tell you,' Pepe said, as if he had reached a decision. 'I will tell you all. What I think happened. When we were about to leave El Lobitos after calling there, our passenger, Señor O'Higgins, is ill. He asked me to take a small parcel for him to Santiago. He will collect it later when he arrives. There were two small parcels, tied together with string.'

'And you agreed to do this?'

'Yes. There seemed no harm in it.'

'I supposed he paid you to do this?' accused Biggles.

Pepe looked shamefaced. 'He gave me a hundred *escudos*, may God forgive me.'

'That was naughty of you, Pepe. Now you think there may have been a bomb in the parcel?'

'Yes.'

'For what reason?'

Pepe shrugged. 'To stop the plane from arriving at Santiago, I suppose.'

'Why?'

'I cannot imagine, unless it was something to do with Atu-Hua, of which I knew nothing at the time. I remember now the manner of Señor O'Higgins seemed strange. He was so anxious for the parcel to go. He said it contained only a clock.'

'And you believed that?'

'Of course. I could hear the clock ticking.'

'Now you think it was the timing device to fire the bomb.'

'Yes.'

'Where did you put it?'

'With other parcels and the mail in the luggage hold. I deserve to be punished for doing such a thing, which is against regulations.'

'You have been punished already,' Biggles said. 'If I were you I would say nothing of this to anyone until you have had time to think about it. It could cause more trouble.'

'It shall be as you say, señor.' Pepe went on, his eyes on Biggles' face. 'Now do you think perhaps Atu-Hua had something to do with all this?'

'Yes, although not in the way you may think. The idol itself could not have caused the plane to crash. To suppose that would be ridiculous, although there may be people superstitious enough to imagine it. I think it was because Atu-Hua was in the plane that a bomb was put on board.'

'But why, señor? Why?'

'Someone did not want Atu-Hua to arrive in Santiago. What other reason could there be?'

'This I do not understand.'

'To tell the truth neither do I, although I now catch a glimmer of light in the mystery. Look at it like this. As far as we know only three people were aware that this religious relic was on its way back to Chile. Someone wanted it there. Someone else did not, and he must have had what he thought was a good reason since he was prepared to destroy the plane and kill everyone in it to prevent its arrival. He must imagine he has succeeded.'

'Now you have the idol, what will you do with it?'

'I shall give it to the man to whom it belongs, the man who bought it in England.'

'The Indians may think it is their property,' put in Conchita.

'That is a dispute someone else can settle.'

'It may be of more value to the Indians than anyone else,' Pepe said.

'Some people, for political reasons, may think otherwise. With the political aspect I am not concerned. Nor is it the concern of the people who sent me here. To them it is, like so many other things today, a matter of money. Atu-Hua was insured in London for a very large sum of money, and unless the idol is recovered the insurance will have to be paid.'

Pepe nodded. 'Ah! Now I understand. Which of the men knew Atu-Hua was in the plane would put a bomb on board? Can you tell me that, señor?'

'No, I can't; but I may find out in time.'

'It must have been the man who paid me to take a parcel to Santiago.'

'So it would seem, but it would be wise not to jump to conclusions. And here I must give you a warning. It may be that the person responsible will not be pleased to hear you have been rescued and so able to tell the story of what happened on the flight. He may try to prevent you from talking.'

Pepe's eyes opened wide. 'You mean I may be in danger?'

'Both you and Conchita.'

'Is it possible?'

'Yes. I can tell you that someone in Chile tried to prevent me from looking for the *Caravana*. Now I have found it, I shall not be popular, either. But never mind about that. The important thing is to get both of you home.'

'And you will take Atu-Hua?' queried Conchita.

'Yes.'

'If it was left to me I'd heave him into the gorge, where no one would ever be likely to see him again,' advised Algy, coldly.

'I think that would be a very good idea, but I don't feel justified in chucking away a hundred thousand pounds of someone else's money,' replied Biggles. 'Having gone so far, we'll see the business through.'

So the day wore on, Algy going outside from time to time to see what the weather was doing. Pepe made no secret of his fear that the Indians would return to look for him, and Atu-Hua. Unfortunately the high priest, or witch-doctor, or whatever he was, got away. 'I saw him go,' he said. 'These were like no other Indians I ever saw; nor did they speak the *Quechua* language common to many Indians of the Cordillera.'

After a pause Pepe went on. 'There's nothing really re-markable about this. There have always been tales and rumours of lost tribes living their lives outside the civilized world, in some remote, undiscovered *quebrada*, in the heart of the mountains.'

'What's a *quebrada*?' asked Algy.

'You'd call it a ravine, or a narrow valley. Why shouldn't there be such places in a mountainous country as big as this? There would almost certainly be some of the original inhabitants who retreated before the gold-mad white men. Some people are of the opinion there are still small parties of Incas who fled to the mountains when they heard that their king, Atahulpa, had been murdered by Pizarro, and a wholesale massacre was going on. This is a matter of history. Now I think I may have seen some of these myself. I could understand some of the words they used, words that have passed into the Spanish language, but not all. They do not live in *chozas*, as we call primitive native houses, but stone places that must have been built long ago. What about the *Moro-chucos*? No one had ever heard of them until a few years ago when a few suddenly appeared in a town in the *Montana*. They said they were the descendants of fugitives, part Spanish and part Indian, who took to the hills to escape after the war of 1824. Such people would manage to live in a country like this, where you can find forest, and grass growing like a *pampa*, up to twelve thousand feet or more; this place we are now, for instance. But I talk too much,' concluded Pepe apologetically.

Algy went again to look at the weather. So far he had always reported 'no change', but now, with evening closing in, he was able to say there seemed to be a little movement in the air and the mist was slowly drifting away.

'The change has come too late in the day to do us any good,' Biggles said, shaking his head. 'I'm not going to try to get off this perch till I can see what I'm doing. It would be better to play safe and wait till the morning. We'll have something to eat and sleep on it.'

With this decision everyone, having flying experience, agreed.

Algy went through to the store locker to sort out a few tins to provide an evening meal, but soon came back with a curious expression on his face. 'Am I imagining things or can I hear something?' he said, looking at Biggles.

Biggles did not answer at once. He went to the cabin door, opened it, looked out, and leaving it open came back. 'You're right,' he told Algy. 'You could hear something.'

'What is it – a storm coming?' asked Conchita anxiously.

'I shall not try to deceive you,' Biggles answered. 'It sounds like Indians bawling their heads off, and I fancy they're coming this way.'

'Now they've got over their fright they're coming back to look for Atu-Hua,' declared Pepe.

'Possibly; or they may be looking for you,' Biggles pointed out.

'What are we going to do?' cried Conchita in alarm.

'There doesn't seem to be much we *can* do,' answered Biggles.

CHAPTER 14

BIGGLES TAKES A CHANCE

THE mist continued slowly, as if reluctant, to disperse, as twilight took possession of the plateau; but as Biggles had said, this improvement in the weather conditions had come too late to be of service to them. The boundaries of the open ground, notably on the cliff side, were no more than vague shadows. To attempt to get the machine off the ground, surrounded as it was by towering peaks running up to twenty thousand feet or more, would obviously be fraught with risks that no experienced air pilot would take.

Noises of what sounded like a barbaric procession, after a pause, were resumed, and clearly were coming nearer. Biggles, who had been standing by the open door of the cabin, conveyed the unwelcome news to the rest of the party that he thought the Indians had now left the wreck of the ill-fated *Caravana* and were now coming up to the plateau.

'I do not understand this,' Pepe said, looking puzzled as well as worried. 'Why do they come here? It is not possible they should know we are here.'

'They know someone is here,' Biggles replied bluntly. 'In that soft ground between here and the crash we must have left a track that a half-blind man could follow on a dark night – never mind an Indian who spends half his life track-ing animals. No one can be blamed for that. It was un-avoidable.'

'Well, we'd soon better be doing *something*,' averred Algy tersely. 'We can't just sit here like tame chickens waiting to have their necks wrung.'

'I think I'll walk along to meet them to find out what all the fuss is about,' decided Biggles.

'What good will that do? You can't talk to them. You can't speak their language,' Algy pointed out with some asperity. 'You go down there and you'll be the first to get a spear stuck in you.'

'It may come to that if we simply sit here and wait for them to come to us,' argued Biggles. 'I've always found it's a good plan to take a bull by the horns and snatch the advan-tage of surprise. When I appear it'll give them a shock. They won't know what to make of me. While they're trying to work it out I may induce them to turn back.'

'Take Atu-Hua with you and give it to them,' suggested Conchita. 'Perhaps that is what they're looking for.'

'I don't think that's the answer,' returned Biggles. 'It might work, on the other hand it might have the reverse effect than the one we want. What do you think, Pepe? I'm open to suggestions. You should know more about these wild men than I do.'

'When I last saw them they were about to throw me on a bonfire,' Pepe said grimly. 'That's the sort of people they are. I doubt if their brains, what little they have, ever get out of low gear. You could shoot some of them. That is something they would understand.'

Biggles looked shocked. 'That's pretty good, coming from you, a Chilean. These people may be Indians, but it doesn't alter the fact that they're Chilean subjects just as much as you are. The colour of their skin doesn't alter that. I've no more right to kill one of them than shoot a white man in Santiago.'

'That is a matter of opinion. If a man tries to kill you, you have every right to kill him.'

'They haven't tried to kill us – yet.'

'The chances are they will. If we wait for that it will be too late to do anything about it.'

Biggles smiled wanly. 'I shan't try to argue against that. What sort of weapons do they have?'

'I only saw spears and stone clubs and axes.'

'No firearms?'

'I didn't see one. Where would they get a gun? I doubt if they've ever seen one.'

'If we don't soon do something they'll be here,' put in Algy, dispassionately.

This was too self-evident to be disputed. 'One thing we *can't* do is let them interfere with the machine,' Biggles said. 'If we lose that we're here for keeps. I'll see what I can do. You keep under cover. Pepe, on no account let them see you. It may have got into their heads that in some way you were responsible for the explosion that scorched their hides.' Biggles turned back towards the door.

'I'll come with you,' Algy said, starting up. 'I'm not letting you go down to face that mob alone.'

'Thanks all the same, but you'll stay here,' replied Biggles, curtly. 'That's an order.'

Algy shrugged, but said nothing.

Biggles went on. 'If I don't come back I can only suggest you defend the machine for as long as you can. But don't start shooting until you have to; by which I mean you've no alternative if you're to try to save your lives. There should be a spare gun in the locker. Give it to Pepe. He'd better keep the last bullet for Conchita, unless she'd prefer to fall into their hands alive with the prospect of spending the rest of her life in the jungle.' So saying Biggles went on to the door and stepped out.

For a minute he stood still, listening to the approaching babble, and judged that it was not far from where the forest thinned out to the open ground of the plateau.

He hesitated as a thought struck him, a factor so obvious that he wondered why it hadn't occurred to him before. All along he had taken it for granted that the Indians knew about, and were in fact familiar with, the god they had once worshipped. Atu-Hua. They would therefore recognize him if they saw him. It seemed this had happened. Pepe's story practically confirmed it. Yet how could that be? Not one of these wild men, whatever their origin, could possibly have seen the idol. Why should they recognize it? How *could* they recognize it? According to the history of the thing it must have been in England for many years, perhaps centuries, before suddenly turning up in the East End of London. That being so, not one of these Indians could have been born when the image disappeared from South America, probably, according to some learned men, on board a Spanish ship returning to Europe.

Biggles' analytical mind raced on. There was something very queer about that. There must be something wrong somewhere. True, the Indians might know about Atu-Hua from hearsay, the story being passed down from one generation to another as so often happens in the folk-lore of any country, be it civilized or otherwise. Yes, pondered Biggles, there was something odd about that. They might know about the god, but that did not mean they would be able to recognize it if they saw it. He was annoyed that this had not dawned on him earlier. It could have made a lot of difference to the way he had handled his investigations, particularly his conversation with Pallimo and Barrendo. What was it Pallimo had said? He didn't particularly want the idol himself, but he was anxious no one else should have it. This now took on a new significance. The reason hinted at by Mr Thurburn in Santiago had seemed reasonable at the time, but now Biggles was not so sure he was right. He became more and more convinced that he had become involved in a plot, a conspiracy, deeper and more sinister than he had suspected.

For a moment he was tempted to change his mind and take the idol with him to see what effect it would have on the clamour still approaching; but he dismissed the idea, the reason being that there was no time to be lost if he was to intercept the mob before it burst on to the plateau and saw the aircraft standing there. After what had happened when they had set fire to the wrecked *Caravana*, he thought they would think twice before they tried to burn the *Merlin*; but there was no knowing what they would do.

Biggles hesitated no longer, but set off at a brisk walk to meet the hubbub now close at hand. He did not draw his pistol, but left it handy in his pocket.

It so happened that he reached the fringe of the forest, where the big trees broke down to a tangle of evergreen tropical shrubs, about a minute before the Indians emerged at the same spot. They were led by a weird-looking creature swathed in rags and decorated with sundry primitive objects. Of course, they saw him standing there, and their behaviour was much as he thought it might be. They came to a dead stop. The noise ended like a pop-playing radio switched off in the middle of a song. They stared, goggle-eyed as the saying is, jaws sagging, faces expressionless in the manner of natives the world over when suddenly confronted with something beyond their understanding. The party numbered about a dozen.

For perhaps half a minute Biggles returned their gaze without moving; but there had to be an end to this. He decided to break the spell. What he did was raise a hand, palm forward, in what in civilization is generally taken as a 'stop' sign, although elsewhere it can be interpreted as a greeting.

It had not the slightest effect. The Indians did not move, except that some who had lagged behind inched forward to see what had caused the hold-up. When they saw the reason, they, too, appeared to take root in the ground. There was not a sound. Thus the scene remained for what must have been a full minute, as if it had been posed for a 'still' movie picture.

Biggles, having no means of communication, could only stand there and wait for the picture to come to life. He was satisfied that so far the natives had shown no signs of hostility, although what they would do when their brains began to work might be a different matter.

The time came when he felt he had better do something, and he resolved on an experiment which he thought could do no harm if it did no good. He pointed at the track by which the Indians had reached the plateau and said in a loud clear voice, 'Go.' He did not expect this to be understood, and apparently it wasn't, for nobody moved so much as a muscle. The Indians continued to stare. He tried the same word in Spanish. The result was precisely the same.

Finding the situation becoming trying he took another line, one from which he thought he might learn something, although it could involve a certain risk. Raising his voice he said 'Atu-Hua.' The Indians might have been stone deaf for all the notice they took.

Deciding that this pantomime had gone on long enough, and might go on a lot longer, Biggles thought the time had come to take more drastic action. He didn't feel like standing there indefinitely; besides, it was getting cold. He took out his pistol. This, judging from the men whose faces were still fixed on him in an unwinking stare, meant nothing. Pointing the weapon well over their heads he squeezed the trigger.

This, evidently, did mean something, for it succeeded in its purpose beyond his expectations. At the flash and the report pandemonium broke out. The entire party, moving as one man, turned about and plunged back into the forest in panic flight. In seconds there was not a soul in sight. A crashing of bushes indicated the head-long nature of the retreat.

Biggles relaxed at this ridiculous anti-climax, put the pistol in his pocket and lit a cigarette. He waited for a minute to make sure the Indians had really gone, and then, turning to go back to the *Merlin* saw Algy running towards him gun in hand.

'I don't think you'll need that,' he said, as Algy came up.

'What happened?'

'Nothing.'

'I heard a shot!'

'We stood staring at each other for so long that finding it getting monotonous I fired a shot over their heads. That did it. One shot was enough. They departed as if I was the devil himself.'

Algy breathed a sigh of relief. 'Good work. Where are they now?'

'Somewhere in the forest. They may not stop running till they get to their village, but I don't think it would be wise to count on that. When they've had time to think about it they may come back for another look. Anyhow, they've gone for the time being. If they'll stay where they belong till the sun comes up in the morning we should be okay. Let's get back to the machine.'

'So they can't know anything about firearms.'

'I wouldn't expect them to in a place like this. In fact, I gambled on that, and it came off.'

As they made their way back to the aircraft Biggles said: 'What has just happened here has given me cause to have second thoughts about this entire set-up. I'm beginning to wonder if I started off on the wrong foot. Either we've been dished out with a parcel of lies, or the people we've spoken to, who are supposed to be experts in local affairs, don't really know what they're talking about. I'd make a small bet that these wretched Indians we've got tangled up with don't know anything about a god, or anyone else, called Atu-Hua. The name, when I tried it on them, produced no more result than if I had said Charley's Aunt. In fact, living as they do, tucked away in the middle of nowhere, I'd go as far as to wager they don't know the first thing about what's going on in the world today. Maybe they're lucky, at that.'

'So what does it add up to?'

'If some smart guy is reckoning on starting a native up-rising by producing this long-lost miracle-worker named Atu-Hua, which I've always suspected was at the root of this fuss, he's likely to find himself up the creek without a paddle.'

'Then why did these fellows start a song and dance when they found Atu-Hua in the wreck of the *Caravana*?' Algy wanted to know.

'If I know anything about unsophisticated natives they jump at the chance to make a song and dance about any-thing. After all, the poor devils don't have much in the way of entertainment. Any excuse will serve for a kick-up.'

'The question is, then, will they come back?'

'That's one I shan't try to answer. Your guess is as good as mine. But for the sake of the loss of a few hours sleep we'd better keep a look-out. If they do come they may not make as much noise as they did last time.'

Algy said no more.

They walked on through the fast-deepening gloom.

CHAPTER 15

A STRANGER INTERVENES

BIGGLES and Algy arrived back at the *Merlin* to find Pepe and Conchita in a state of acute anxiety.

'What happens?' asked Conchita, breathlessly.

'Nothing,' Biggles told her.

'You met them?'

'Of course.'

'What did they do?'

'Nothing.'

'Where are they now?'

'Gone home, I hope.'

'I heard a shot,' Pepe said.

'I fired one over their heads to discourage them from coming any farther.'

'Did it?'

'Yes.'

'What happened?' asked Conchita.

'They stampeded back into the forest. Let's hope they stay there.'

'Will they?'

'That, dear lady, is something I don't know,' Biggles answered patiently. 'We can only wait to see. How's your leg?'

'Better, thank you.'

'Good. Then let's have something to eat. There was one thing about the fog. If it kept us here it prevented anyone from coming to see what had become of us.'

Nothing more was said. Algy prepared a simple meal from the emergency store locker. Conchita helped him, a task for which, as an air hostess, she was qualified. Biggles went out to check on the weather and returned with the information that the sky was clearing. There was still a little light mist clinging to the plateau. During the meal he went to the door two or three times to listen for ominous sounds from the direction of the forest, but each time he returned to say that everything was quiet. The air was still, and cold. The meal finished and cleared up, Algy offered to take first watch.

Biggles agreed. 'Wake me at midnight,' he said. 'I'll finish the night and have everyone awake at the crack of dawn ready for departure.'

'Is it necessary for someone to sit up?' asked Conchita.

'To be on the safe side, yes,' answered Biggles.

'And if the Indians come?'

'We will deal with that if it should happen.'

Algy went to the open door and took up a position on the step. The others selected seats and made themselves as comfortable as the situation allowed; which was, in fact, in the roomy cabin, fairly comfortable. Silence fell. Biggles was soon asleep.

He was still asleep, as were the others, when Algy roused him by pressure on the shoulder. 'Your watch,' he whispered.

'Anything doing?'

'Nothing. Can't hear a sound.'

'Good. Sleep well.' Quietly, so as not to awake the others, Biggles went to the door and stepped out to survey the scene before taking up the position Algy had vacated. It was dark. Well, comparatively dark, for the sky, now clear of mist, was ablaze with stars so bright that they did not appear to be stuck to the dome of heaven, as in more northern climates, but hung suspended in space – as, of course, in fact they were. Even with the moon absent they gave sufficient light for the plateau to be bathed in a cold luminosity not of this earth. The gorge below the plateau was a bottomless well filled with mysterious shadows. The air, at this altitude, was thin, and chill. Biggles took a long, penetrating look, in the direction of the forest, and listened for a minute. The silence was absolute. He might have had the world to himself. But he had experienced this sort of phenomenon before and gave no thought to it. Seeing nothing and hearing nothing, he settled down for his self-imposed vigil.

Time passed. A long time. He did not make it seem longer by looking constantly at his watch, knowing that the glow in the sky of the false dawn would tell him that the time had come to rouse the others in preparation for departure. Inevitably, in these conditions, although he remained alert he sank into a reverie, pondering the problem he was trying to unravel, turning over in his mind such evidence as he had in an endeavour to find the vital clue which he was sure must exist: something that would spotlight on the whole peculiar business. The only conclusion he reached was, whoever had put the bomb in the *Caravana* it was certainly not Pallimo, because he had been thousands of miles away, in England, when the aircraft had taken off on the last stage of its journey to Santiago.

From the pensive state of mind into which he had fallen as a result of his speculations, he was jerked to the present by a sound so remote from reality that for an instant he feared he must have dozed off and imagined, or dreamed, it. It was a

cry. It had appeared to come from the direction of the forest.
A voice had called, in Spanish: 'Hello there.'

Biggles stood up, staring into the gloom. He did not
answer. What sort of nonsense was this? He could see
nothing. Had he really heard something? The cracking
of broken twigs confirmed that he had. Presently the
call was repeated, followed this time by 'Where are
you?'

Still Biggles did not answer. Thinking fast, he decided
that the words had not been spoken by an Indian, although
that was not impossible. He derived some comfort from the
obvious fact that this was not a stealthy approach. Whoever
the caller might be, he was announcing his presence in no
uncertain manner. The thought occurred to him that it
might be the captain of the *Caravana*, or his second pilot,
who, according to Conchita, had set off for help. Could they
have found their way back to the scene of the crash? It
seemed unlikely, but he could think of no other possible sol-
ution.

A minute passed. In the solemn hush it became possible to
hear someone moving; approaching. He focused his eyes in
the direction of the sound and waited, motionless and silent.
Presently he could just make out the vague outline of a
figure advancing slowly through the patch of lilies, or whatever the flowers were, that flourished on the fringe of the
trees. It stopped. Again came the cry. 'Hello!' There was a
pause as if the caller was waiting for a reply. Receiving none,
he continued to advance.

After giving the matter urgent consideration, Biggles now
answered. 'Hello! Over here.' This said he waited, tense,
watching the figure, without any attempt at concealment,
coming towards him. By this time he judged the man should
be able to see the starlight shining on the plain surfaces of

the aircraft. But he was taking no chances. When the man was within twenty paces he said curtly, unthinkingly, or perhaps naturally, in his own language: 'That's close enough.'

This produced another shock of surprise, for the reply came instantly, in English, 'Say, are you an American?'

'No, English,' Biggles answered.

'English! What in the name of glory are you doing here?' The voice had a strong North American accent.

'That's my business,' said Biggles stiffly. 'I might ask you that question. What do you want?'

'To get away from here,' the man went on. 'Do we have to shout at each other? You scared of something?'

'Yes,' returned Biggles frankly.

'Well, you've no cause to be afraid of me.'

'Are you an American?'

'No. Chilean.'

'Then why do you talk like an American?'

'I was some years in the United States. Aren't you going to invite me in and give me a drink?'

'Not yet. But you can come a bit closer.'

'Oh hell! You can trust me.'

'I'm not in the mood to trust anyone.'

The man moved forward. At the same time, Algy, apparently awakened by the talking, said from behind: 'What the devil's going on here?'

'We have a visitor,' Biggles told him shortly. Then, to the man. 'That's near enough. Who are you? What's your name?'

'Estiban Huerta.'

'From where?'

'Santiago.'

'What are you doing here?'

'If you'll let me sit down and give me a drink I'll tell you. I've just had a rough time.'

'All right. You can come in. No tricks.'

'The last thing I'm likely to do, brother, is play tricks. Just help me to get out of this, that's all I want.'

'Have you been with the Indians?'

'Sure. I've just managed to get away.'

'Are they likely to follow you here?'

'I don't think so. Not from what I heard them saying.'

'Does that mean you can speak their language?'

'More or less. I've been here before.'

By this time Pepe and Conchita were awake and standing just inside the cabin door to see what was going on. They moved back to allow Biggles, Algy and the stranger, to enter. Algy put on a light as they sat down, so it was now possible to see the stranger properly for the first time.

He was a man perhaps in the early thirties with a lean figure and a sun-tanned face, lined from exposure or possibly recurrent fever. His hair was black, long and matted; his chin unshaven, showing the beginning of a beard.

'What in the name of creation are you going here?' he asked, as Algy handed him a drink.

Biggles answered. 'Never mind what we're doing here. What are you doing in a place like this, apparently by your-self? Who were you calling?'

'I didn't know. Anyone.'

'So you knew someone was here?'

'Sure.'

'How?'

'From the Indians. Now you'll want to know what I was doing with the Indians, so if you'll listen instead of asking questions, I'll tell you.'

'Go ahead. We're listening.'

'First, let me explain I'm a prospector, a bit of an explorer, too. That came from reading too many adventure books when I was a boy. All I ever wanted to do was to go looking for adventures, and believe you me I've had my share. When I was old enough my father, who lived in Santiago, sent me to college in the United States. I studied, and took a degree in metallurgy. I knew what I was going to do. I also knew that in these mountains there must be plenty of precious metals. So, when I came home, and my father had died, I quietly packed a rucksack and set off to find some of them.'

'Alone?'

'Sure. I didn't want a partner to get in my way. What I was really looking for, of course, was adventures. The sort of adventures I'd been reading about. For a time I made a living collecting chinchilla pelts on the high tops – you know, those little grey rats that have one of the most valuable skins in –'

'We know about *chinchillas*,' interrupted Biggles. 'Go on.'

'Well, that's what first brought me in contact with the Indians. I got to know them and they got to know me. I got to know more and more of them as I explored places where no one else ever went. Such as here. I learned to speak their languages. These Indians here are an offshoot of the Araucanians. They never go near civilization. I was able to give learned societies, and the government, a lot of information about them. That brought me into contact with certain people who were interested in them.'

Biggles looked at the speaker. 'Who, for instance?'

'Well, there's a man, a rich man, named Pallimo. In fact, it was he who sent me here.'

'He *sent* you here?'

'Sure.'

'To do what?'

'Well, it seems he'd heard that someone was spreading a rumour among the Indians that one of their ancient gods was coming back to them, to help them.'

'And what were you supposed to do?'

'Find out if it was true and who was spreading this report.'

'Are you talking about a god named Atu-Hua?' asked Biggles quietly.

The stranger stared. 'Sure. How the heck did you know?'

'I came here on a similar errand. To find out if Atu-Hua did come back. If you don't already know, it may interest you to know that he did.'

'Like hell he did!'

'What's that supposed to mean?'

'How do you know he came here?'

'I've seen him. As a matter of fact he's here – in this plane.'

'Forget it. Have you had a good look at him?'

'I haven't examined him, if that's what you mean. Why?'

'Someone has sold you a pup. I've seen what you've got. It's a fake. A copy. Not a very good one, either. The thing you've got is a lump of carved soapstone with a piece of cut red glass stuck in his face.'

It was Biggles' turn to stare. 'How did you know it was a fake?'

'I didn't. But the Indians knew. Don't ask me how they knew. But the headman of the tribe was never in any doubt about it. That's what started the trouble. In the ordinary way these people are quiet enough. But they were expecting the real thing. Now they think it's another trick by white men to fool them like their ancestors were fooled. They even turned on me.'

Biggles caught Algy's eye. 'At last we seem to be getting somewhere,' he murmured.

CHAPTER 16

A TAKE-OFF TO
REMEMBER

LOOKING at the lone explorer Biggles went on. 'Atu-Hua
turned up in London. It was sold. Pallimo bought it. He put
it on a plane for Santiago. The plane carrying it –'

'Crashed in the forest just below us here. I know all about
that.'

'Where do you suppose the genuine article is now?'

'I'd say Pallimo has still got it. It was never on the plane.
He didn't want the Indians to have it.'

'How do you know that?'

'He told me so. He thought it might start trouble. That's
why he offered to pay me a thousand *escudos* if I'd do a tour
of this part of the country to say it was all lies about Atu-
Hua coming back. He knew no one knew the Indians as I did
and that I could speak their language. I'd been here, before,
prospecting for gold. There was no trouble then, nor at first
this time when I first arrived. I did what I was sent to do.
Then came the crash and I was in the soup up to the
neck.'

'They found Atu-Hua.'

'I've told you what they found. The witch-doctor wasn't
fooled. He raved, calling me a liar and a cheat. He had me

tied up. Tonight I managed to get free and made for here. That's the story.'

Biggles nodded. 'I believe you. Tell me. What do you make of all this? Have you any idea of who might start a rumour that Atu-Hua was coming back?'

Huerta thought for a moment. 'I know only one man who understands the Indians anything like as well as I do. He's been around quite a lot and he's well up in local affairs. His name's O'Higgins.'

'O'Higgins, eh?' Again Biggles glanced at Algy. 'Why should he start a rumour that Atu-Hua was coming back?'

'I didn't say he did. But he's interested in the Indians. He came to see me two or three times when I was in Santiago. He seems to have a bee in his bonnet about the original inhabitants of the country. He collects relics of them, particularly objects connected with the old religions.'

'Such as Atu-Hua?'

'Sure.'

'If he had the original he could produce it any time it suited him.'

'I suppose so. Anything else you want to know?'

'You've told me plenty to get on with. We shall have to try to sort it out when we get back to Santiago. You try to get a nap. I'll see what things are like outside.' Biggles beckoned to Algy and walked to the door. Algy followed him. They found everything still quiet, with the stars fading in the light of a rising moon.

'To me this whole business gets murkier and murkier,' Algy said. 'I can't make head nor tail of it. Who do you reckon has got the original Atu-Hua?'

'I'd say Pallimo still has it.'

'What?' Algy's voice indicated incredulity.

'You heard me. That's what I think.'

'Where is it now, then?'

'Presumably at his home in Santiago, since he's returned from London.'

'But it was he who started all this bother. That doesn't make sense to me.'

'Then let's see if we can make it make sense. This is how it seems to me in view of what Pepe has told us and what this chap Huerta has just said. I'll admit my theory is based on conjecture; but where evidence is lacking we have nothing else to work on. I may be wrong, but this is how I see it now.' Biggles broke off to light a cigarette.

He resumed. 'When the idol was sold there were three men in London who had a more than ordinary interest in it. Pallimo, Barrendo and O'Higgins. They all wanted it. Barrendo, you remember, told us he wanted to buy it, but was outbid by Pallimo at the sale.'

'But why did these men want it so badly?' asked Algy, wonderingly.

'Because here the thing would become a symbol of power over the native population; and apparently for one reason or another they're all interested in politics. Pallimo, having secured Atu-Hua by means of his wealth, was afraid one of the other two might try to grab him. He told me he trusted O'Higgins implicitly. I don't believe it. Men of his calibre trust nobody. Maybe that's why they get rich. Being political opponents, it's unlikely that any of these men trusted the others. They've all been playing a deep game. But that isn't really the point. Having bought the idol, Pallimo's concern was to get it home. He decided to lay a false trail. What he did was go to a sculptor in London and have a cheap replica made.'

'What makes you think it was Pallimo who had the copy made?'

'He was the only man with the original; the only one of the three who could get the work done within a certain time limit. Put it like this. Neither of the others could have had a copy made until Pallimo had handed the thing over to O'Higgins, and by that time they were booked to go home. Had either of the others wanted a copy, it would have had to be made *en route*, and that isn't feasible. No. That copy must have been made in London, by Pallimo. He then contacted O'Higgins and asked him to take Atu-Hua with him when he went home to Santiago. What he gave him, of course, was not the genuine article but the fake. I can see reasons for this. If O'Higgins stole the fake idol and tried to use it to his advantage, Pallimo could prove him a cheat by producing the real thing. The genuine god might even be used as a sort of blackmail. Be that as it may, O'Higgins set off for home with the copy, leaving Pallimo to follow in his own time with the authentic Atu-Hua. Are you still with me?'

'Yes.'

'Right. Let's go on, although we can only surmise. Barendo finds out that O'Higgins is taking a parcel home for Pallimo and guesses what is in it. Or O'Higgins might have told him. He hadn't given up hope of getting Atu-Hua, so he books a passage on the same plane. What happened on the early part of the trip we can only guess, but we can be certain of one thing. These two men, the only passengers, knowing each other, would talk. What would they be most likely to talk about? Atu-Hua. They may have had a peep at the contents of the parcel. If they did they must have realized that the thing with them was a fake and Pallimo had pulled a fast one on them. That may be why Barrendo wasted no more of his time on it, but decided to leave the plane at Buenos Aires.'

'Leaving O'Higgins to go on alone.'

'Naturally, he would be furious at having been fooled by Pallimo and would try to think of a plan to get even with him. Knowing the plane could land at El Lobitos, he decided to beat Pallimo at his own game by seeing the plane never arrived in Santiago. So he planted a bomb on board with the dud god. Pepe has told us how he did it and the excuse he made for leaving the flight at El Lobitos.'

'I don't get it,' Algy said. 'What good would sabotaging the plane do him?'

'We can still only guess what was in his mind. For one thing he'd be in a position to prevent Pallimo from claiming the insurance money.'

'How?'

'By declaring the whole thing was a fraud. Atu-Hua was never on board. The object he was carrying was a copy connived by Pallimo. If the wreck of the *Caravana* was ever found it could be proved. Pallimo would never be able to produce the real thing without incriminating himself. I know this sounds complicated and hard to believe, but we must remember that these men we're talking about would be unscrupulous in politics.'

'A bunch of crooks,' sneered Algy.

'I didn't say that. In the ordinary way they might be perfectly honest men, loyal and patriotic. But this is politics, with each man doing what he thought was best for the country.'

Algy looked aghast. 'According to you O'Higgins was prepared to murder the crew of the *Caravana*.'

'Why not? They meant nothing to him in view of what was at stake. When it comes to political power there have been men who thought nothing of starting a revolution knowing that innocent people would lose their lives. It still goes on. Things haven't changed.'

'These men are all now back home. What are you going to do?'

'I shall think about that on the way to Santiago. Frankly, I don't care what these men do to each other. We were sent here to scotch an unsubstantiated insurance claim and that's what I intend to do.'

'How?'

'Probably by meeting Pallimo face to face and having it out with him. He was at the bottom of the whole thing by faking the copy of Atu-Hua. We have it. I'll hear what he has to say about that.' Biggles glanced up at the sky. 'Here comes tomorrow,' he observed. 'In half an hour it should be light enough for us to get away.'

'Just a minute,' Algy said, striking a listening attitude. 'Can I hear something?'

From some distance off, below, in the forest, there came a sound like the buzzing of a swarm of angry bees.

'Sounds like the Indians getting worked up again,' Biggles said. 'They're coming this way.'

'Why here?'

'I wouldn't know. They may be looking for Pepe or Huerta – or anyone else to have a go at. They'll know Huerta must have come this way. But instead of talking we'd better get cracking. Let's get the others moving.'

'But you can't see to get off yet.'

If the worst comes to the worst I shall have to try. We can't start a pitched battle. They're still some way off. The light will be better by the time they get here. Anyway, we'll get all set to go.'

Those in the cabin were roused and the position explained to them. This caused alarm but no panic. The *Merlin* was already in position to take off, so nothing more could be done. Biggles told Algy to stand outside to keep watch and warn him as soon as the Indians came into sight. If they stopped when they saw the aircraft they might gain a few more valuable minutes, but if they came on he was to get aboard at once. Having told those in the cabin to hold tight if he had to take off, as the ground might be bumpy, he took up his usual position in the cockpit, started the engines to allow them to warm up and then sat back peering through the windscreen. He could just make out the vague mass of the cliff on the left, and on the other side the blank space where the plateau ended on the lip of the gorge.

Outside suddenly, the babble of the Indians ended abruptly, and he could only guess that they had seen the aircraft and were staring at it. The silence did not last long. It ended in a wild medley of yells. Algy shouted, 'They're coming – they've got spears,' and climbed into his place beside Biggles. He slammed the door. 'Buck up,' he said urgently. 'They're close.'

'Fasten your belt and hang on,' ordered Biggles grimly, at the same time easing open the throttle. The voices of the engines rose to a bellow as the *Merlin* moved forward, fast gathering speed.

Algy, staring ahead, could only pray that the machine would gather flying speed before it came to the end of the plateau, still lost in gloom. Of just what happened during the next minute he was never afterwards quite sure. The aircraft bumped rather badly, as it was bound to on such rough ground, although the bumps became less severe once the tail had lifted. Biggles managed to keep a straight line. Then one of the undercarriage wheels seemed to strike something hard, causing the machine to swerve off its track and run at an angle towards the chasm that yawned like a bottomless pit to the right of them. There was no time to recover from the jolt even if this had been possible without wrenching off the undercarriage. The *Merlin* tore on. It shot over the edge and plunged down into a world of mist and shadows. The engines died as Biggles cut them.

Algy made no sound, but clapped his hands over his face to wait for what he naturally supposed would be the end of the plane and everyone in it. It did not come. Pressure in his seat told him the inherent stability of the aircraft was bringing its nose up, as if recovering from a stall. When he thought they were on even keel, and dared to look, he saw they were in thick mist, Biggles rigid in his seat taking the machine up in a gentle climb. He couldn't remember the depth of the gorge, if he had ever tried to judge it, but obviously there had been room for the *Merlin* to recover from the stall before hitting the bottom.

'You'll kill me,' he managed to gasp.

'There's still time for that,' answered Biggles crisply, looking down, and then, swiftly, to left and right. 'We're well down in the valley. From what I remember of it there should be room for us to get out.' It was soon revealed that there was. Climbing more steeply now as the engines developed their full thrust, the *Merlin* suddenly burst out into sunshine under a blue sky. Algy breathed again.

'Check if they're all right inside,' Biggles said.

Algy did so, and returned to say all was well except that the passengers were suffering from shock.

'I'm not surprised. So am I,' was the answer.

Still climbing, Biggles took up a course through the towering snow-clad peaks that confronted them. There was no more trouble.

Half an hour later the *Merlin* was in soft, warmer air, making the long glide down over the fertile valleys of the central zone towards its temporary base at Los Cerrillos.

Here Biggles asked Algy to take over for a minute and went aft into the cabin.

To the two men and the woman he had rescued he said: 'I want to ask a favour of you. Presently we shall be landing and you will have to make your own way home. I have some important business in Santiago in connection with the *Caravana*, so you'd oblige me by saying as little as possible about what has happened until tomorrow, when, of course, you will have to make your official reports on the crash.'

This being agreed, he returned to the cockpit and a few minutes later was landing at the airport.

CHAPTER 17

BIGGLES PLAYS THE LAST CARD

LATER the same day, at their hotel, after a meal, a clean-up and a short rest, Biggles told Algy what he had made up his mind to do. 'I'm going to see Pallimo right away,' he announced.

'Why not wait till tomorrow?'

'He may not be here tomorrow. When the story of what happened to the *Caravana*, and his association with it, leaks out, as it's bound to, he might think it prudent to make another trip abroad until the fuss dies down. Sooner or later Pepe and Conchita will have to make a full report, and it's right that they should; and you can't keep a story like that out of the newspapers. I want to catch Pallimo before he hears any details.'

'What do you hope to do?'

'Get from him a written admission that he still has Atu-Hua, or knows where it is. With that in my pocket he'd never dare to make a claim for the insurance money. That's all I'm concerned about. It's all the Air Commodore wants. I'm as anxious to get home as you are; before the balloon goes up, as it will. I'd rather not be involved. If there's an official inquiry, as probably there will be unless Pallimo has enough power to hush the whole thing up, we might be kept hanging about here for months. The three people in the case, Pallimo, Barrendo and O'Higgins, can fight it out among themselves. That's why I'm going to act now, before things start to boil over.'

'Then what? Do you want me to come with you?' Algy asked.

'No. Knowing what these people are capable of, I'd rather play safe and keep an escape route open. If I know anything, with his reputation at stake Pallimo would go to any lengths to get his hands on proof of his participation in the Atu-Hua affair. I mean that spurious god he had made. If anything should happen to me, and you'll know that it has if I don't come back tonight, you'll go to the airport, collect the machine, and taking the fake idol with you – it's still in the locker where I put it – make flat out for home by yourself. Hand the thing to the Chief. That should be enough evidence to knock on the head any claim for the insurance. While I'm out you can get the *Merlin*'s tanks topped up ready for off. Then come back here and wait for me.'

'Okay, if that's how you want it,' agreed Algy. 'And if Pallimo admits the truth?'

'We'll start for home first thing in the morning.'

'If there's an inquiry you'll be expected to be here to give evidence.'

'If the owners of the *Caravana* want a report from me they can get it through official channels in London.'

'Fair enough.'

That was all. Biggles went out, called a taxi and gave the address of Pallimo's residence. On arrival he ordered the driver to wait, and going to the door announced himself, saying he wished to see Señor Pallimo urgently. This must have aroused Pallimo's curiosity, for he was not kept waiting.

He was shown into a room richly furnished with antique Spanish furniture. The man he had come to see came forward to greet him affably, which gave Biggles reason to think he had not yet heard anything about the *Caravana*.

'This is a pleasant surprise, Inspector,' he said. 'I'm happy to see you. I heard you were here. Have you had any luck?'

'You may not be so happy when you've heard what I've come to see you about, sir,' Biggles answered coolly.

Pallimo's expression changed. 'Indeed? Don't say you've managed to find the missing *Caravana*?'

'I have. I've also found the fake Atu-Hua you gave O'Higgins to bring home.' Here, of course, Biggles was firing a shot in the dark; but judging from Pallimo's expression it hit the mark.

Pallimo frowned. After a pause he said: 'I don't know what you're talking about.'

Biggles retorted. 'Señor Pallimo, you don't want me to tell you a story which you must know as well as I do, perhaps better. The object you gave O'Higgins to bring home was a copy of the original.'

'How do you know?'

'I found it and brought it back with me.'

Pallimo sat down. 'Where did you find it?'

'In the wreck of the *Caravana*, which someone sabotaged by putting a bomb on board.'

'I wasn't responsible for that,' stated Pallimo, quickly.

'I didn't say you were. But someone was, and it cost several people their lives. For that, if only indirectly, you were responsible.'

Pallimo poured himself a drink with a hand that was not quite steady. He offered one to Biggles, who declined. 'What are you going to do about this?'

'That depends on you.'

'What do you want?'

'Have you still got the original Atu-Hua?'

Pallimo got up again. 'Now, Inspector, we can settle this unfortunate matter amicably, I'm sure. We don't want a public scandal. I could make it worth your while –'

Biggles shook his head. 'No. You've got the wrong man, señor. You haven't answered my question.'

'Frankly, yes, I have it.'

'Where is it?'

'Here.'

'That's all I want to know. Let me make my position clear. I've no wish to be the cause of trouble here. Why you did what you did I don't know, but I can guess. My mission here was simply to make sure that a fraudulent claim was not made for an object alleged to be lost. There my interest ends, so I am prepared to make an arrangement with you.'

'What do you suggest?'

'All you have to do is give me a document saying you still have Atu-Hua. That will prevent any claim being made for the insurance.'

'And if I refuse?'

'The dummy you had made will go to London as evidence of the fraud. That would mean exposure, not only in London, but here.'

Pallimo thought for a moment. 'If I give you such a document what guarantee have I that you won't publish the story in –'

'No guarantee at all. You'll have to take my word for it. But if you don't comply with my request I may have to talk. There are one or two other details you should know. I found, rescued from the Indians who were holding him prisoner, and brought him home, a man I believe you know. His name is Huerta. He told me he was employed by you to undertake certain work among the Indians. I also brought home two survivors of the crash. A radio-officer and an air hostess. They can tell you what happened. You'll have to make your own arrangements with them. Incidentally, the two pilots of the plane are still missing.'

Still Pallimo hesitated. 'Are you going to stay on here?'

'Give me the document I want and I undertake to be out of the country within twelve hours, taking it with me.'

Apparently this decided Pallimo. He walked to a writing desk and picked up a pen. 'Very well,' he said. 'What exactly do you want me to say?'

'You can write at my dictation. I'll keep it short.'

'As you wish.'

Biggles dictated, Pallimo writing.

'I, Don Carlos Ricardo Pallimo, of Santiago de Chile, hereby state that the jade statue of the god Atu-Hua, which I thought had been lost, has been recovered and is in my possession. I therefore withdraw unreservedly any claims to compensation for its loss.'

'Now sign it,' Biggles said.

Pallimo signed, blotted the document and handed it to Biggles who put it in his breast pocket. 'Thank you,' he acknowledged. 'As that, Señor Pallimo, concludes our business, I won't detain you any longer.'

'I'm sorry about this, Inspector,' Pallimo said contritely. 'I meant no harm. I acted for the best. I employ a great many Indians and would not like to see them induced to cause trouble to suit someone's political aspirations. It was foolish and wrong of me. I can see that now.'

'We can all make mistakes, señor,' answered Biggles, as they walked to the door. 'Good night, sir.'

'Good night, Inspector.'

Biggles found his taxi waiting and was driven back to the hotel.

'Well?' queried Algy.

'No bother at all,' informed Biggles. 'I have his confession in my pocket. He isn't really a bad man. He tried to get away with something, but this time it didn't come off. We'll leave for home at the crack of dawn.'

The rest of this curious case can be left to the reader's imagination. There was no more trouble, much to Biggles' relief, for he was afraid that Pallimo, when he had had time to think, might change his mind, and with the power at his disposal might try to prevent them from leaving the country. However, this did not happen, and sunrise the next day saw the *Merlin* in the air, climbing steeply to surmount the stupendous barrier that rose between it and the broad plains of Argentina.

Two days later Biggles and Algy were in England. Biggles went straight to the Air Commodore's office and put on his desk Pallimo's confession and the false little green god. 'I think these are all you will require, sir,' he reported.

'Did you have any trouble?'

'Not really.'

'Good,' said the Air Commodore. 'Join me for lunch and you can tell me how you did it.'

Biggles never learned the outcome of the affair of the Little Green God, although it must be admitted that he never went to any trouble to find out. He was not sufficiently interested to inquire. Being a purely domestic matter, nothing appeared in the Press outside Chile. He had done what he had been sent to do and was content to let it end at that. He did hear, however, weeks later, from a chance meeting with a pilot of the *Caravana* company, that the matter had been taken to court, but even he did not know who was suing whom, or for what.

One detail that reached his ears, one that pleased him, came in a letter of thanks from Conchita; she thought he would be interested to know that the two pilots of the missing *Caravana*, who had gone for help, had eventually turned up in Argentina. As a postscript she added that she was also writing on behalf of Pepe, whom she had married.

So why the various parties concerned with the ancient god Atu-Hua, had behaved as they had, remained something of a mystery. There appeared to be little sense in it; but as Biggles remarked to Algy when they were discussing the case some time later, he never could make much sense out of foreign politics, anyway.

STAMP COLLECTING

Stanley Phillips

The Stanley Gibbons standard work on stamp
collecting, now for the first time in paperback.
Revised and brought up-to-date with new
material and with 16 pages of photographs.
Contents include: The story of the post –
stamp designing and printing – overprints –
colours – postmarks – forgeries – the outfit –
how to get and identify stamps – arranging
the collection – different kinds of collection –
the stamp world – treasure trove.
With an appendix covering stamp currencies –
philatelic terms in three languages – stamp
inscriptions translated – the meaning of
overprints.

MEET THE PEANUTS GANG

DON'T TREAD ON CHARLIE BROWN

WHAT WERE YOU SAYING
CHARLIE BROWN?

Charles M. Schultz

If you haven't met the Peanuts gang before,
now's your chance to get acquainted with
Charlie Brown and his friends (not forgetting
Snoopy the dog) who have made such a hit
in this country and the United States.
And if you are already a Peanuts fan, these
books contain some of the earlier cartoons
which you probably won't have seen before.